Edward William Bok

Beecher memorial

Contemporaneous tributes to the memory of Henry Ward Beecher

Edward William Bok

Beecher memorial
Contemporaneous tributes to the memory of Henry Ward Beecher

ISBN/EAN: 9783337141684

Printed in Europe, USA, Canada, Australia, Japan

Cover: Foto ©Raphael Reischuk / pixelio.de

More available books at **www.hansebooks.com**

Religion without Superstition,
Government without Tyranny, and
regulated freedom To all people.

Henry Ward Beecher

Brooklyn, N.Y. }
Plymouth Church. }

1884 —

BEECHER MEMORIAL

CONTEMPORANEOUS TRIBUTES

TO THE

MEMORY OF HENRY WARD BEECHER

COMPILED AND EDITED BY

EDWARD W. BOK

PRIVATELY PRINTED
BROOKLYN, NEW YORK
1887

THE DE VINNE PRESS.

INDEX OF CONTRIBUTORS.

HENRY WARD BEECHER.

HIS MANY-SIDED CHARACTER AND GENIUS.

REMINISCENCES AND INCIDENTS.

NOTE.

The acknowledgments of the Editor are due to the many distinguished contributors to this Memorial for the cordiality with which his request for their coöperation has in every instance been received, and the cheerful readiness which has characterized each response. His indebtedness is likewise acknowledged to Major James B. Pond, for many years Mr. Beecher's warm and trusted friend, and to Mr. William J. Bok, his fellow-worker in this labor of love.

The cordial assistance and approval of Mrs. Henry Ward Beecher and of Colonel William C. Beecher are also gratefully acknowledged.

E. W. B.

BROOKLYN, June 1, 1887.

INTRODUCTION.

HENRY WARD BEECHER was the purest type of the robust free American. He was born in New England, and there received his early education. But he studied theology in Ohio, and at the age of twenty-four commenced preaching in Indiana, when that State was part of the "wild West," and there he preached for ten years. This had much to do in shaping his ideas, and in giving such boundless freedom to the expression of his thoughts.

We all believe in the blood of horses and dogs, and it has always seemed to me that heredity in man was likely to be governed by much the same laws. With Mr. Beecher this appeared especially true. His compact muscle, his remarkable physique, his impulsive nature, and his vital force were pure inheritances from that ancestry of which he was ever proud. He acted out his nature, and whatever he did was done easily, because naturally. He never tried to be a polished scholar, nor did he aim to be careful about the delicate conventionalities of aristocratic life. If he had been bred in England, he would have been a power at the hustings or in the House of Commons. But Henry Ward Beecher sitting, in bishop's robes with lawn sleeves, in the House of Lords would not have seemed at home.

His fertility of intellect was amazing. For full fifty years he talked to the public, and no man ever said so much and repeated himself so little. His humor was immense, as any one who looked into his face could see. He was of an artistic temperament, and would have made a great actor. He had a vast heart, with broad benevolence flowing over the human race. He loved men, women, and children, of whatever race or creed. His personal magnetism made him interesting always. His combustion was spontaneous. He was at his best when with blind allonge he threw himself into the tempest of his thoughts. He read much and rapidly, and observed all sorts of men, women, and things. He stored his mind more by observation than by study or *reflection. I do not think he ever did reflect; he* FELT. *He talked and acted as he was impelled to talk and act. He was never restrained in his utterances by the least concern about subsequent criticism. He used words to express his thoughts. He once told me that he was like the "town pump," dry in summer, needing to wait the autumn rains before he could pour out a full stream.*

Mr. Beecher's imagination was large; his hope was boundless. Kind and sympathetic to the last degree, he wished well to the world generally. He abhorred oppression everywhere, was resolute without caution, and could conceal nothing. He was always to be found on the side of liberty, humanity, and equal rights. He liked to call things by their right names. He hated the word "kleptomania." He was told of a rich woman who stole costly laces from a counter,— the shopkeeper said nothing, but sent his bill to her husband with a polite note. Not many days afterward, a poor woman stole a little cheap frock for her child, and was sent to prison. The one act was called "kleptomania," the other "larceny." This exasperated Mr. Beecher beyond measure.

The brave and efficient services which Henry Ward Beecher rendered in the cause of imperiled freedom, both in England and America, when our skies were darkest, need not here be dwelt upon. They will be forever gratefully remembered by all good men, and pass into the imperishable history of the time.

If, in the Judgment Hall, Osiris weighs all the deeds of men, he will find a heavy balance of good to the credit of Henry Ward Beecher.

The following memorial to this illustrious man, to which so many eminent persons have contributed, may fitly serve to perpetuate the memory of one of the most gifted products of free government in America.

EDWARDS PIERREPONT.

New York City.

William H Beard.

Living, above the clouds he soared:
From realms of upper air
His mighty eloquence he poured—
Dying, he lingers there.

WILLIAM H. BEARD.

IN MEMORIAM

HENRY WARD BEECHER

DR. OLIVER WENDELL HOLMES.

ONE is not likely to forget the day when he first saw Henry Ward Beecher. I first met the great speaker and teacher at Pittsfield, Massachusetts, somewhere about the year 1855,— a little later or earlier perhaps. He came there to preach on the day of the week which at home I had heard called Sunday, and at Andover and in other rural districts " the Sabbath." Though the day was not known in our Cambridge household by its false Jewish name, it was observed in the old Puritan fashion. On Saturday playthings were put away at " sundown," all voices were hushed, and all features subdued and sobered. I had never got over the saddening effect of this early discipline : indeed, I have hardly recovered from it to this day. When Mr. Beecher appeared on Sunday at Pittsfield, joyous and radiant, it seemed as if the leaden cloud which had hung over the day for so many years had given way to a burst of sunshine. No long faces, no melancholy tones, no fear of a smile, or even a laugh, no constraint, but, on the contrary, a wholesome, natural, cheerful welcome to the day of rest. He moved as briskly as if it were a week-day, talked as pleasantly as if it were a holiday, was good-natured, not worrying over his sermon, playful at times ; in short, was himself,— one of God's happy, strong, useful servants and sons, who really believed that his Maker was a kind and reasonable Father.

In the pulpit, Mr. Beecher was the same unaffected, robust, out-spoken, clear-headed, sensible man, with a gift of fervid eloquence and a power of effective illustration which swayed the multitudes before him as the wind sways the leaves of the forest. He never addressed men as if they were convicts, born rebels, and would-be devils, but as brothers, to be helped, to be led, to be raised upward into the higher atmosphere of good thoughts and good companion-ship. What a comfort it was, after hearing a bloodless invalid preaching "as a dying man to dying men," to hear a sound, strong-bodied, healthy minister of the Gospel speak with virile force and ringing accents, as a *living* man to *living* men ! I never forgot that Sunday. He did more than any other preacher had ever done to exorcise the demon of dullness who had brooded over the day ever since my childhood.

Nobody could help knowing something of the Plymouth pulpit. Mr. Beecher's sermons went all over the land, and reached the members of a congregation which Saint Peter's could not have held had it been twenty times as large. So much of himself as he did not expend in sermons, addresses, essays, books, he gave out in talk which was listened to as eagerly as ever were the responses of an ancient oracle. There seemed to be no end of his productive-ness. It is easy to criticise his methods and to find fault with his rhetoric. He represented a great natural force as truly as does the boiling stream of a geyser. Of course he may have been sometimes uncomfortably hot to meddle with, though one of the best-tempered men in the world ; of course he sometimes shot up into extrava-gance, but the heat that drove forth his impassioned utterances came from " the burning depths below." He was a mighty power in the land,—not a *talent* but a *puissance*, as was said of Berryer.

It is of little consequence whether a man like Whitefield or Beecher leaves behind him any monumental literary work to carry his name down to a remote posterity ;— his work was on the life around him, and its results can never be known until the books of heaven are balanced.

Mr. Beecher was as genuine an American as ever walked through a field of Indian corn. He had not the fine fiber of the scholastic thoroughbred, but he had the hearty manhood which we knew in Lincoln, the accumulated vitality which reveals itself from time to time in mighty natures, never more fully, perhaps, than in that of Webster.

What Mr. Beecher did for the country during the war of secession no man can estimate. I ventured to say in 1864, speaking of his work in England :

" In point of fact, this unofficial visit of a private citizen in connection with these addresses delivered to miscellaneous crowds by an envoy *not* extraordinary and a minister *nulli*potentiary, for all that his credentials showed, was an event of national importance. It was much more than this,—it was the beginning of a new order of things in the relations of nations to each other."

If the popular orators whom the Old World sends to this country all came on errands as holy as was that of Mr. Beecher, we should feel much happier about the " new order of things," as illustrated in the missions of the apostles of anarchy and crime.

Few men have had such burdens laid upon them as those which Henry Ward Beecher had to bear during his long and eventful life, and he has borne them like a man. His fresh, just-finished record is a wonderful story of a life of almost unexampled activity. The characters in which the story is traced may fade out,— they must fade out, like other traces of past lives; but moral force, like physical, is indestructible, and the impulse given by his labors in the cause of humanity will live unsuspected in far-reaching and imperishable influences.

OLIVER WENDELL HOLMES.

Boston.

GENERAL WILLIAM T. SHERMAN.

THE friendship existing between Henry Ward Beecher and myself was most warm. We met often at the festal board and on the platform, and I recall our wanderings together over the plains and in the mountains of California and Oregon. His greeting was always so hearty, so full of manly vigor, so outspoken, that he seemed to me more like an army comrade than a minister of the Gospel. And these two characters are not inconsistent, for Christ himself assumed the form and speech of men to go into closer relation and thereby influence them for good. Though Brooklyn claimed him as her own, Henry Ward Beecher was too large a man for any single locality. He was essentially a national man grasping all the thoughts and feelings of a continent, storing his mind with the beauties of the sea-coast, the vast campaign fields of the interior, and the wild forests and cliffs of the Rocky Mountains, thereby illustrating his discourses by vivid pictures of the glories of the universe. His mind and imagination could not be tied down to the narrow dogmas which shackled smaller men, and I am not surprised but rejoiced to know that he occasionally kicked over the traces. My last meeting with Mr. Beecher was at the house of Dr. Talmage, and he seemed then so strong that I believed he was destined to outlive me. But he has gone, having attained the full measure of three-score years and ten, and has left behind a name and fame which should satisfy his family, and writings which will carry hope and consolation to millions.

W. T. SHERMAN.

New York City.

THE RIGHT HON. WILLIAM E. GLADSTONE, M. P.

I THINK it a high compliment to be invited to contribute to the series of memorial writings in honor of Rev. Ward Beecher, and I assure you that if I ask to be excused from that duty it is only because I am aware that I have not the knowledge, direct and personal, which alone could enable me to discharge it worthily. I never had the good fortune to meet Mr. Ward Beecher but twice, and on neither occasion was I in close personal intercourse with him.

To his undying fame the world and his memory stand in no need of witnesses, and those who stood within the circle of his friendship will, I have no doubt, bear ample and weighty tributes to his character and wonderful genius.

I ought to add that I am very grateful for the remarkable but too indulgent notices so frequently bestowed upon me by Mr. Beecher.

W. E. GLADSTONE.

London.

ADMIRAL DAVID D. PORTER.

FEW men have performed so faithfully the labors he assumed as Mr. Beecher. Whether in the capacity of theologian, orator, lecturer, or citizen, his life marks an era in the history of our country, and his vacant place is not likely to be filled. When I saw Mr. Beecher in the pulpit, or in any other position where he brought his oratorical powers into play, I could compare him only to the mighty falls of Niagara, sweeping everything before it. He was sovereign among orators, as Niagara dominates all other cataracts. He was the Himalaya, overtopping all others of his profession ; the leviathan, compared with whom the common herd are but as a shoal of minnows ; and although there are many occupants of the pulpit, men of high aspirations and brilliant talents, yet none of them can fill the vacancy. " None but himself can be his parallel."

In the pulpit, Mr. Beecher occupied the place held in the forum by Daniel Webster, and his great talents were only exceeded by his benevolence. It was simply necessary to look into his face to see how full of sympathy and kindness was his heart, and should any question arise, his account-books would show the thousands of dollars spent upon the needy.

When I first saw Mr. Beecher's benevolent face and leonine head, I said to myself, " What a grand man that is ! " but when I heard him speak, it was as if a mighty river was rushing through my soul washing out every vestige of sin abiding there, and I think I was a better man after listening to that sermon. Twice did I hear him, and I would have attended Plymouth Church regularly had I lived in its neighborhood.

The gifts with which nature had endowed our great pulpit orator were never used to better purpose than when he made his pilgrimage to England during our civil war, to plead the cause of the Union and battle against the prejudices of our transatlantic brethren. For his services on this occasion, the people of the United States owe to Henry Ward Beecher an eternal debt of gratitude.

The death of this great Christian orator is an event that will long be remembered. It is only necessary to recall the weeping throngs who attended his funeral to realize how he was appreciated by those who knew him best, and the floral offerings laid upon his coffin were tributes of affection such as few men have ever received.

Henry Ward Beecher was a great national character, and as such will always be remembered. He was ever ready to devote all his energies to the service of his country, and had it been necessary, I doubt not but that he would have shouldered a musket in her defense.

DAVID D. PORTER.

Washington.

THE POET WHITTIER.

OF Henry Ward Beecher as a reformer and orator, and as a great moral and political force in his day and generation, no words of mine are needed. Our country owes him a deeper debt of gratitude than it has paid or can ever pay him for his noble services in the dark days of the Rebellion. One of the bravest of men, he proved the truth of the adage that the bravest are the tenderest. Apart from his unequaled pulpit successes, his bold and efficient advocacy of temperance and the abolition of slavery entitle him to the grateful remembrance of the nation and of all mankind.

JOHN GREENLEAF WHITTIER.

Oak Knoll, Danvers, Mass.

RIGHT REV. FREDERIC W. FARRAR, D. D., F. R. S.

I ONLY saw Mr. Beecher once, so that my acquaintance with him was of the slightest. I once heard him preach at Brooklyn, and once heard him lecture in London. It would have been impossible for any one to hear him without being struck by his great power. I have very rarely listened to any man who seemed to have a more powerful hold upon his audience, or a more generous sympathy with all sorts and conditions of men of every race under the sun.

FREDERIC W. FARRAR.

Westminster, London.

SONNET.

"It is a good thing to work for immediate returns; but that is the lowest form of a man's working. Work for the invisible."—HENRY WARD BEECHER.

How vast a brotherhood doth mourn this man,
  Who held all men right, brotherly, and dear,
Or were they free or bond, dwelt far or near,
Exalt in place, or bowed beneath a ban!
Heart-vision made him great; the under-plan
Of God's loved world to this so loving seer,
As in a sunbright prospect did appear,
Toward which his fleet warm hopes forever ran.

All ye his brothers! well he wrought for you;
And for the invisible in you he wrought,
Truth's fields and sacred Freedom's battles fought.
Into the invisible he late withdrew,
Yet still works here, though lost to outward view,
Kindling from heart to heart high-missioned thought.

EDITH M. THOMAS.

Geneva, Ohio.

REV. ROBERT COLLYER, D. D.

I CAN give no better estimate of Henry Ward Beecher than by saying that he suited me in all respects. His work in the religious life of this country was very great. What Tasso said of his instructor may be said of Mr. Beecher: he was like a whetstone, for all that came in contact with it were able to put a fine edge on their tools. We are all brighter from contact with pure souls, and so we were when brought in contact with Henry Ward Beecher. To my mind he was the greatest preacher on this planet, and had been since he arrived at the fullness of his life. His thought will not die with him, though it may become absorbed in other minds, but never in books. His mind was like fine wheat sown to spring in new harvests. His living spirit cannot die. Men will be his debtors for ages to come, as he did so much in these plastic times, when all things are so fluent. One great thing in his character was that, with all the advance he made as a pioneer of new truth and new life, he never lost sight of the settlement in which his brethren lived. Then he had such an inexhaustible fund of things to say, illustrations pouring out of his mind as rivers pour their tides down to the ocean, and never running dry. A great many sermons are like a glass of Missouri water,—you must let it stand and settle before you can drink; very often you will have to throw half away. But the sermons that Henry Ward Beecher preached were translucent, fresh, and pure as spring water.

ROBERT COLLYER.

New York City.

MR. EDWIN BOOTH.

IT was my misfortune never to have met our great countryman Mr. Beecher, but many years ago, on one of the saddest occasions of my life, he sent me a message of such hope and encouragement that I have ever held him in grateful and affectionate esteem. Were it in my power to add the merest leaf to his hardly-won and well-merited olive wreath, I would gladly do so ; but, alas ! I can offer to his family and his friends only my profound sympathy.

EDWIN BOOTH.

San Francisco.

GENERAL JOHN C. FRÉMONT.

IT is to me one of the satisfactions which stay in a man's life, to have had the friendship and support of Mr. Beecher in some of the contests through which this country has fought its way upward during the generation which has just closed. The aid which he then gave was not merely an influence, but the support of a crystallized opinion which surrounded him and moved with him. Of this kind was the aid he gave to the preliminary struggle of the

Northern people in 1856, and his public and emphatic approval given to the proclamation of freedom in the early part of the civil war.

It was in connection with these events that I knew him best. Like Mr. Calhoun, if Mr. Beecher had been in political life, he would have been the leader not of a party but rather of a sect devoted and unquestioning. If his life had been cast in Southern Europe or Asia, he would have been a great prophet and swayed nations. He had the strong personality and the vivid eloquence which rouse men to the enthusiasm that controls events.

In later years I had rarely met him. The intercourse with all the world, growing yearly more intimate, brings before us daily such a concourse of events to demand attention that our friends occupy less space, and I have only had passing glimpses of his actions and opinions. These all went to show how incessantly and deeply his mind was dwelling upon the great truths and the great myste- ries to the elucidation of which he devoted his life.

Not often do the tidings which bring to our unwilling ears the extinction of a great life leave behind them such deep regret and pity. But the record of his noble life is now immovable. He has crossed over the " narrow frith " to the obscure immensity which the efforts of his tireless mind lost itself in seeking to penetrate, and now in the searching light of that further shore where all is known he stands, at rest, before Him who is infinite in love.

J. C. FRÉMONT.

Washington.

MRS. JAMES A. GARFIELD.

IT was my privilege a few times to listen to Mr. Beecher, and the memory of his earnest words, of the lessons they taught, and the encouragement they gave will abide with me an inspiration forever. To his generation has he been a grand example of heroic devotion to the search for truth ; a brave exponent of the high principles he professed in character worthy of the world's respect and veneration, and of him now can it be truly said, " He being dead, yet speaketh."

LUCRETIA R. GARFIELD.

Mentor, Ohio.

THE PASTOR'S FAREWELL.

THE sermon was o'er — the prayer — the song —
    And dimmed was the mellow light ;
With summer at heart, the homeward throng
    Went out in the winter night.

But the pastor staid, at his tired heart's choice,
    To list to the chanted word ;
For the organ-loft and the human voice
    Still sung to the pastor's Lord.

The sweet tones brought to his wearied heart
    Their mingled smiles and tears ;
And he felt that night full loath to part
    From the shrine of forty years.

The scene of a thousand wondrous hours
    He saw, as he glanced around ;
The vase of affection's faithful flowers —
    The blood of a battle-ground.

'Twas here he had preached with tones of love,
    Or the clarion call of strife.
Of God within, as well as above,
    And sweetened the bread of life.

And here, with gesture of brave command
    And tenderly beaming face,
He had reached to the world a thrilling hand,
    And fought for the human race.

'Twas here, with a strength by anguish bought
    And a love that never slept,
He rocked the cradle of new-born thought,
    While the century smiled and wept.

He saw the thousands that o'er this track
    Had walked to the country of day ;
And now they seemed to be reaching back,
    And beckoning him away.

But ere long time his soul had been
        By olden memories stirred,
Two boys from the street came wandering in,
        To list to the chanted word.

Two young, fresh hearts, with a goodly sum
        Of innocence' saving leaven,
Like such it is said ours must become
        Before we can enter heaven.

They heard in silence, with face upturned,
        And tremulous, deep surprise,
And all the fire of the music burned
        Within their youthful eyes.

There crept to the old man's eyes a mist ;
        And down the pulpit stair
He gently came, and tenderly kissed
        The children lingering there.

And o'er their shoulders his arms he threw,
        This king with the crown of gray,
And finally, like three comrades true,
        Together they walked away.

And two went out in the winter night,
        Their earth-toil just begun ;
The other, forth to eternal light,
        His work for the planet done.

                                WILL CARLETON.
Brooklyn.

HON. JOHN SHERMAN.

So many eloquent and able tributes to the memory of Henry Ward
 Beecher have already been written, presenting his wonderful
life and great career in language so eloquent, that when I under-
take to add to these eulogies my pen falls from my hand, and I feel
that anything I might write would only be a repetition of words and

ideas printed before in more glowing language, and by friends who knew him better than I. These eulogies detail his wonderful career as preacher, lecturer, orator, humanitarian, journalist, and citizen in so full and attractive a shape, that no one could be at a loss in placing Henry Ward Beecher as one of the greatest, if not the greatest, of the men of our times, with a warm heart for every human being, with genuine sympathy for all who suffered injustice, and with an intellectual power and an address that made him the most successful preacher and the most striking orator of his day.

Mr. Beecher has now closed the record of his life, and the passion and prejudice of his contests while living are passing away, so that we can feel and express without limit our admiration and affection for him. Generous, brave, and sympathetic, a hater of falsehood, he was also a man of the highest intellectual ability and culture. Believing, as I heartily do, that the good will be rewarded in a future life, I have faith that Henry Ward Beecher will take his place in the world of spirits, and there enjoy " that vast and bright eternity—all vivid with God's love—in which an instant vision shall be perfect joy, and an immortal labor shall be to him immortal rest."

JOHN SHERMAN.

Washington.

HIS GRACE, THE DUKE OF ARGYLL.

MY regret is sincere that my personal acquaintance with Mr. Beecher was far too limited to enable me or entitle me to express any opinion except in his character as a public man. Moreover, even in this aspect I have no direct knowledge of anything except the prominent part he took in the great contest against slavery in the United States. In this matter he did noble work,— work as noble as that done by his illustrious sister, my old friend, Mrs. Harriet Beecher Stowe. These two names will be held in everlasting remembrance by all who value the efforts of genius in a noble cause.

ARGYLL.

Argyll Lodge, London.

REV. W. H. H. MURRAY.

ABRAHAM LINCOLN emancipated men's bodies; Henry Ward Beecher emancipated their minds. The one delivered them from injustice; the other, from superstition. The one was buried amid the tears of his countrymen; the other, with the admiring tributes of mankind. Both were the gift of God. The one, that America might be free; the other, that Christendom might be enlightened. I mourned over Lincoln's grave as over the saviour of Liberty, dead; I mourn over the going of Beecher as at the departure of a seer of God.

To Henry Ward Beecher were given eyes that were not born of the flesh, nor limited, as to their power, by the capacity of the senses: eyes that saw through and within the circumference even to the center of things; that saw the long parallels of truth without contraction, and so ever beheld unfolding before them the wide horizons of God, and not a mere point of human determining. He looked, and he saw; he gazed, and beheld; and what had been hidden to others, to him was revealed. For he saw as none ever saw, save the seers of God, the hidden and sweet things of Life Everlasting.

And to this power of vision was added a voice,—a voice that said to the eyes. "I will tell what you see, whether men hear or forbear," and it did; and for years it sang and it thundered. And men hearing trembled or wept, laughed, or cheered the voice that none might resist, for the power of judgment, of honor, and of tenderest love was in it.

Nay, Beecher, I say not farewell! For thou art not gone, but only vanished. Our eyes shall see thee again, and our ears shall hear the song of thy lips, even wiser than ever, and our hearts shall feel the beating of thine and glow as of old, for thou art teacher and prophet of God for ever and ever, and we and all men are thy pupils. So, I say not farewell, as do many, but rather " Good speed, and far-going!" Thou art flying a new flight, and with wings that tire not thou art speeding and looking and learning. Thou art seeing strange sights and wide views, and over deep depths art thou poising, and beyond thee are heights,—thou shall reach them! And with thee fly many who are wise and far-sighted: the seers of all ages and the prophets of all peoples, and by them thou art taught, and them thou art teaching of God, many-named, but One only.

Good speed, good speed! say we then. Thou art gone, but we follow. For by and by toiling onward awhile and then mounting upward, we will come,—we with many,—and then thou shalt tell us of all thou hast seen, and teach us again of Mercy and Truth and the Way of Life Everlasting. Good speed, good speed, great soul! Go on and up, ever seeing and learning. We will join thee anon!

WILLIAM HENRY HARRISON MURRAY.

Burlington, Vermont.

MR. ANDREW CARNEGIE.

IN the death of Henry Ward Beecher, America loses its greatest citizen, the world its greatest preacher. The Republic has indeed a few names greater than his upon its century's roll — a very few; but the world's records for all time contains not the name of a greater pulpit orator. The supremely great preacher deals not only with the future life, he proves his power to influence for good the events of this life, in which our duties lie. This attribute of supreme greatness Mr. Beecher fully shares with Savonarola, Becket, Richelieu, and Knox; and it is this which raises him and sets him upon a pedestal apart from any preacher of his time.

It was not my privilege to know this great man with the intimacy which brings into view the common infirmities of humanity. It was in his great moods, when he was at his best, that I beheld him — far enough away, as it were, for the mass and grandeur of the mountain and not its inequalities of surface to show upon the horizon. One felt in his presence that nature had sketched with a free hand and upon broad lines a massive character. Nothing petty, nothing vindictive — a lovable, loving man, brimful and running over with melting charity, all-embracing.

Mr. Beecher must ever remain before us in the twofold character of preacher and statesman. In the former field he was the foremost and most powerful champion of that select band of advanced men who are broadening and deepening the furrows in the hard and barren soil of theology, that the light of the sun and the dews of heaven may penetrate it and make it fertile.

The fame of the orator, like that of the actor, necessarily rests upon tradition ; and in this age when theology has lost its vital hold, the pulpit orator, in particular, rarely makes any contribution to the thoughts of men destined to survive him. His special province, the elucidation of creeds, is scarcely tolerated when the minister is in the flesh, and can adorn the subject with graces of speech and action. That his disquisitions are to be read when he is gone is not to be expected. But Mr. Beecher's influence upon theology is nevertheless destined to be permanent ; for he was a revolutionary force in the ecclesiastical field.

It is, however, in his capacity as statesman that he is to be longest and most gratefully remembered. Here he not only indicated, but in great measure dictated, the policy of the State in the greatest crisis of its history. The most powerful voice in the struggle with slavery was his, and his, too, the position in the front. Always pointing unerringly the next step which the patriot had to take — never doubting, never faltering, never waiting, but always indicating the only true path to safety ; preaching a holy crusade against slavery, insisting that only through the removal of the guilt could the terrible struggle end. Henry Ward Beecher was the inspired prophet of the land — at once the Moses and Joshua of our exodus from the thralls of bondage to the fair heights of freedom. And having raised the masses at home to the height of the great contest, he went forth to appeal to the democracy of England to stay the hand of aristocracy eager to strike at republican institutions in the hour of trial.

Few Americans fill the world with their name ; but there is not a community in the civilized world where the name of Henry Ward Beecher is unknown. No one can hesitate to pronounce him a genius. The essence of genius is that it sits, solitary and alone, upon a throne of its own creation. We have one Shakespeare and one Burns. The world is never to see another of either. We have in Beecher one who resembles them in this : that as he was without prototype, he is to remain without successor.

ANDREW CARNEGIE.

Pittsburgh.

MISS ROSE ELIZABETH CLEVELAND.

THE last time I saw Mr. Beecher was something over one year ago. On that occasion he told me that he had never felt more equal to his work ; that he was then confronting the public, either from pulpit or platform, upon an average of once each day ; that he was conscious in no way of any loss of strength or vigor. His appearance did not belie his words. As he sat, erect and ruddy, talking earnestly of those great themes which were his life-long study, he certainly looked, in his composure of strength, all that he claimed. This was during a short stop he made in Washington on his way to points further South in fulfillment of his engagements. Later on in the season he crossed the ocean, and our mother country felt again, throughout her whole domain, in these his riper years, as before in middle life, the undiminished magnetism of his genius.

Now, in the seclusion of a country hamlet, untouched by that great world in which we last met, I realize at length, after much argument of brain bewildered, and heart wounded, by his sudden taking off, that he has again gone abroad, this time far and forever ; that all his magnificent mortality has dropped from him ; that he will not return to us, and that only as we go to him can we again be in his company. Yet, of what mortal man has it ever been less true to say that he is dead ? To what living spirit has ever been, or would ever be, more exactly fitted those words of St. Paul : " Not . . . . unclothed, but clothed upon, that mortality might be swallowed up of life " ?

It will be long before the last word will be said of Henry Ward Beecher. To take all the testimony as to the fruitage of his life, his love and his labor for his fellows, would be to traverse in all its round area this world of ours (one little spot of which alone could claim to be his home !), and to halt, with recording pen, at many obscure dwellings whose occupants discharge in constant, unrecognized remittances of love and gratitude their life-long debts to him who was their preacher, their teacher, and their friend.

It is well to have this written memorial that it may bear what testimony it can to the memory of this beloved man ; to thus perpetuate some slight expression of the feeling toward him of a very few of those who now rise up to call him blessed. But it is due to

him and to them alike that these favored few who gladly inscribe a
leaf within this volume should realize that we are but as a handful
of grain from the vast stretch of sand that girdles the unfathomed
sea to those who are and who, from the nature of things, must continue to be, if not in every sense the great unknown, yet always
certainly the great unheard-from. Could their voices join ours in
this tribute, there would arise an echo from that chorus which would
knock at the very gate of that heaven into which he of whom we
sing has entered, and perchance steal in a minor yet not discordant
note to that celestial symphony to which his ear is now forever
attuned.

                                      ROSE ELIZABETH CLEVELAND.
Holland Patent, N. Y.

SIGNOR TOMMASO SALVINI.

IN giving utterance to my feelings respecting the Rev. Henry
Ward Beecher I lack, in addition to other difficulties, the par-
amount advantage of having known him personally. I can, therefore, only limit myself to a just appreciation of his fame, rendered
world-wide through the innumerable endowments which distinguished so great a personality. From all those who have had the
good fortune of listening to his oratory, we gather expressions of
profound admiration for the depth and acumen of his philosophical
ideas and universal knowledge : as also for his religious views and
humanitarian principles, which, shaped into words and delivered
with all the mastery of elocution and the charm of the most perfect diction, proclaimed him to be indeed one of the best patterns
of the true apostles of Christ. How many rare qualities, hidden
from public gaze, must they who knew him intimately have had
occasion to observe in so refined and privileged a nature !

It is said that death, being common to all, is a just law, and I
am myself convinced of its equity as a general rule; but it appears
to me most tyrannical when thus wrenching from our midst one
who, still in the main strength of his exalted manhood, was lavish-
ing upon all those around him the inexhaustible treasures of his
unbounded knowledge and wisdom.

2

Anxious though I be to express my deep-laid sympathy to his bereaved family, yet stronger do I feel in me the desire of offering my deepest condolence to the nation for the loss of so illustrious a son,— nay, of mourning with all mankind at large for the place left vacant by so noble and tireless a champion on the path of progress and in the cause of universal good.

TOMMASO SALVINI.

Florence, Italy.

EX-PRESIDENT RUTHERFORD B. HAYES.

THE only time I ever heard William H. Seward in public speech was in Washington, at a meeting of friends of Governor Thomas Corwin, held soon after his death, to take steps for the removal of his remains to their final resting-place at his home in Ohio.

Mr. Seward said: "I concur in all that has been spoken in regard to the eloquence, the wit, the humor, the generosity, the amiability, and the genius of the deceased. Eloquence and every other talent, however, are but instruments in what we do or attempt to do. The question is, what he has done, or what he has attempted to do, for his country and for mankind."

Henry Ward Beecher's career will stand the test suggested by the wise statesman of New York. On the vital questions of his time, at the critical periods, at the very points where the need was the sorest and the hazard the greatest, his talents were all employed on the side of his country and of humanity, with a devotion and courage which Americans will always remember and admire. In the anti-slavery struggle his pen and voice and presence were always at the command of the good but unpopular cause. The cities of New York and Brooklyn had few favors to bestow on the abolitionist. Mr. Beecher knew very well that, with his gifts, popularity, fame, and wealth without stint were at his feet if he would speak only smooth things. But, with a cheerful spirit, he bravely kept the faith, and did his appointed work. During years of almost hopeless struggle he stood by the slave, the type of whatever was humble and lowly and helpless among men.

Again, in the great conflict, when all was at stake, he justly earned
an honored place on the roll of those who served their country best.
Secession had but one chance in the war. Grant that the people of
the North had equal sense, equal patriotism, and equal pluck and
endurance with the people of the South, and the contest might be,
as it was, long and hard indeed, but it could not be doubtful. The
one rational hope of the South was help from Europe. European
intervention depended on England. Her ruling class, as a body,
were against the Union, and were ready to serve the South.
Would public opinion hold them back? This was the question.
Our Government strained every nerve to reach the English mind.
Our best equipped men for such work were sent abroad. Bishop
Mac Ilvaine, Archbishop Hughes, Thurlow Weed, and others were
selected to spread before Great Britain the merits of the cause
of America. In 1863 Mr. Beecher met the English people and
debated before them the critical question. At the beginning his
audiences were stubbornly, violently, and almost unanimously
against him. I need not give the history of his brilliant triumph.
It was complete and overwhelming. In fitting and merited recognition of this wonderful service, the honor was given to Henry
Ward Beecher to replace upon Fort Sumter the flag which Disunion
and Slavery had pulled down.

RUTHERFORD B. HAYES.

Fremont, Ohio.

M. AUGUSTE BARTHOLDI.

I AM too much attached to all that is American not to be touched
with sentiments of sorrow at the death of the illustrious Henry
Ward Beecher. His sublime life cannot but leave its mark upon
the generation which has had the honor and glory to possess it, and
the beneficent influence of his works is destined to be eternally
felt by posterity.

BARTHOLDI.

Paris, France.

REV. T. DE WITT TALMAGE, D. D.

WHEN, amid a congratulatory scene at my house a few days before his death, Mr. Beecher came to me at the close of the evening and said, " I am going now." and I answered, " you shall not go," and he said, with an arch smile, " but I will go." I had no idea that his stay in this world was to be so soon terminated.

Others may speak of Henry Ward Beecher in other relations; I speak of him as a neighbor. Neighboring pastors, sad to say, are not always good friends. Disaffected members cross over from church to church, and the transfer sometimes causes pastoral irritations. But Mr. Beecher had no sympathy with such infinitesimals. He always had a kind word to say of his neighbors, and when he met them was as genial as a morning in June. We met one day on the street in front of a furniture store, chairs and sofas standing outside the door. " Come," said he, " let us sit down here and talk," and so in the street we sat and talked, until the number of spectators and auditors gathered suggested to us that we had better move on. Many a long ride had we together in the rail-cars, going to great distances. His anecdotes never gave out, and we never had so good a time together as when we got into discussions in which we were diametrically opposed. He on the way to Cincinnati, and I on the way to Chicago, while nearing Pittsburgh, he said to me: " Talmage, you don't know anything about mathematics." I said to him, " I know as much about them as you do." So we went into competitive examination on the " multiplication-table," and he tried " eight-times," and broke down, and I tried " nine-times," with similar discomfiture. We then agreed never again to make any allusion to the subject of mathematics.

For nearly nineteen years we worked side by side, and there was never a ripple between us. I shall never have a better neighbor. Although we belonged to different generations, he never took on the patronizing air that the older sometimes shows toward the younger. But he has passed out from among us, and we had all better be busy, since we see that the longest life soon ends—a lesson we learn every day, and forget as soon as we learn it. With his afflicted family we have more sympathy than we can utter, and for Plymouth Church we wish great prosperity. God makes no two men alike, and that church will not expect a repetition of their former pastor; but there are a hundred men that I know, any one of whom could take the pulpit of that church, and from it wield unlimited usefulness.

Realizing that this letter is not the conventional letter written for memorial volumes, I hope nevertheless it may not be an inappropriate expression of admiration for a good neighbor gone forever.

T. DE WITT TALMAGE.

Brooklyn.

MR. GEORGE WILLIAM CURTIS.

THE traditions of Summerfield represent a beautiful youth and a captivating speaker. The charm of Channing was profound and indescribable. But Henry Ward Beecher recalls Whitefield more than any other renowned preacher. Like Whitefield, he was what is known as a man of the people; a man of strong virility, of exuberant vitality, of quick sympathy, of an abounding humor, of a rapid play of poetic imagination, of great fluency of speech; an emotional nature overflowing in ardent expression, of strong convictions, of complete self-confidence; but also not sensitive, nor critical, nor judicial; a hearty, joyous nature, touching ordinary human life at every point, and responsive to every generous moral impulse.

In the pulpit, he inculcated right living, rather than traditional doctrine. He was a soldier of the church militant, but his warfare was with human wrong and misery, and false theories of life, and low aims, and poor ambitions. He aimed to build up righteousness of life, and in the ardor of the strife he liked to pause and wink, and let fly a bright-tipped, winged word at the opponent, against whom he bore no kind of malice. He hated the wrong, but not the wrong-doer. His profession was the preaching of peace and good-will. But how often he must have felt that his Master came not to bring peace, but a sword! His buoyant temperament, his perfect health, his love of nature and of man, of children and flowers, of the changing sky and landscape, his abounding sympathy, his rich and sensitive humor, made his life joyous and often happy. But it was none the less a stormy life, ending at last, amid the sorrow of a country, in happy rest and the good fame of a great orator for human welfare.

GEORGE WILLIAM CURTIS.

West New Brighton, Staten Island.

MR. LAWRENCE BARRETT.

DESPITE the many obstacles that seem to rise before me as I attempt to pen a few words in memory of the great preacher and citizen who has left us, I am nevertheless desirous to be included among those who, with their testimonials in this memorial volume, will testify to the honor which they feel of having lived in the age of Beecher, and who knew the courage which carried him to the front at critical moments in the history of our country, as a leader whom all must follow. I would like to stand among those recorders who can testify to the eloquence which fell spontaneously from his inspired lips, voicing a fearless soul which confronted the narrow dogma in which his youthful soul was swathed with the sublime audacity of his wonderful genius. I am old enough to recall that period of his career when he fell into line with the contemners of the drama, and I rejoiced in the liberality which led him in his later years to confess his early error, and regret that he could have ever been arrayed against the foremost literary influence of all ages.

Through Henry Ward Beecher the century offers the welcoming light of revelation to inspire the teachings of science. The church has been made the better for his life : mankind was an incalculable gainer by it, and his death was a blow which all humanity felt. A place has been made vacant which no living man can fill, and the loss to the nation and to the world, therefore, is irreparable.

LAWRENCE BARRETT.

New York City.

HENRY WARD BEECHER.

PREACHER. PATRIOT. PHILANTHROPIST.

Like a fountain that upsprings
  In a desert wild and drear,
Like a clarion note that rings
  Through the fastnesses of fear ;

Like a fortress on a rock,
  Set to guard a wide domain,
Sheltering the affrighted flock
  When Destruction sweeps the plain ;

Like a storm whose grandeur wild
  Takes its way at heaven's behest ;
Like a Samson undefiled,
  To Untruth a fatal guest :

Thus, with thoughts that flame and soar,
  Thus, with spirit-weaponed hand,
For dear peace and righteous war,
  Stood our preacher in the land.

Gracious nature, graceful art,
  Wove for him their blended crown :
He could bless with brimming heart,
  He could call God's thunder down,

Bitter woes of humankind !
  Sin and sorrow, grief and wrong,
Was he to your beckoning blind ?
  Did he slight you in his song?

And the mystic things of God
  That we dimly apprehend,
Did he tread them, roughly shod,
  Shatter beauties without end ?

I remember well the thrill
  Multitudes were glad to share

When the solemn aisles did fill
  With the music of his prayer :

With his sermon wisely planned,
  Reasoned with a master's might :
Faith's illuminating hand
  Touched its sentences with light.

That we had him is a boon
  That commands a song of praise ;
That we lose him oversoon
  Is a grief for all our days.

Having ? Losing ? All those years
  Pregnant with celestial fire ;
Can we quench them with our tears,
  Like a warrior's funeral pyre ?

No. those treasures dearly bought
  Are beyond the reach of fate ;
They are builded in our thought,
  They are welded in our state.

On the solemn judgment mount
  He, methinks, may fearless stand,
For the final, dread account.
  With his record in his hand.

A great army would attest
  The true succor that he gave
To the poor God loveth best,
  To the woman, to the slave !

He once more may fitly pray
  If a prayer can sound in heaven :
·· Be God's help to me this day,
  As the help that I have given.''

JULIA WARD HOWE.

Boston.

MARCHIONESS ADELAIDE RISTORI DEL GRILLO.

IT is difficult for me to say how much grieved I am at the news of the Rev. Henry Ward Beecher's death. Such a loss is not only a sad blow to his friends, but to mankind, because in him has just passed away one of the most powerful champions of civilization, whose splendid example and inspired words contributed so effectually to the emancipation of the negro. It is with a melancholy satisfaction that I write my regrets with those of all his countrymen, preserving in my heart an indelible remembrance of this true apostle of science, progress, and freedom.

ADELAIDE RISTORI DEL GRILLO.

Rome, Italy.

HON. GEORGE F. EDMUNDS.

WITH no means at hand for a studied review of the life of Henry Ward Beecher, I will nevertheless state my impressions of this remarkable man. They are founded entirely on his career as it was manifested to the public, for I had not the honor of a personal acquaintance with him. Seen in such a light, I think it cannot be doubted that he was a man of intense earnestness and high courage. It seemed as easy for him to breast the currents of popular opinion, and to obstruct the course of hoary tyrannies, as it is for many to float on the changing stream of the one as to be instruments and supporters of the other. His sense of what was meant by liberty among men, and what that liberty really was and must be, unless it were to be a lofty phrase to hide a mass of lies and wrongs (as it now sometimes is), must have been profound, for his voice and influence were devoted to the cause of antislavery when, even in communities legally free, it brought obloquy and not renown.

His visit to England and his work there, in a dark and critical period of the rebellion, when the government and the great body of the ruling classes of that country were exerting all their power (just short of open alliance with the rebel government) to effect the destruction of our republic,— when, as related by Justin McCarthy in his history, Lord Russell was saying that the struggle was one "in which the North were striving for empire and the South for independence," and when William E. Gladstone was declaring that "the President of the Southern Confederation, Mr. Jefferson Davis, had made an army, had made a navy, and, more than that, had made a nation,"— when the Duke of Argyll and John Bright and a very few others were our only open friends,— were a conspicuous example of the lofty and persistent moral courage that seemed to grow more and more bright and daring in proportion to the number of the foes to be overcome.

Another example may be found in his differences with his clerical brethren. Whether we agree or not with his beliefs or propositions, we must render due homage to that independence of thought and brave candor that bore him to warfare against the creeds and traditionary dialectics that appeared to him to separate the individual man from direct and responsible relations with his Creator, and to make his soul's welfare dependent upon the opinion or the belief or the intervention of some other man.

His political conduct also was of the same type. Platforms and candidates no more measured or controlled his action as a citizen than did formulated creeds or rituals his religious responsibilities. Unity and coöperation if possible ; but first and always the duty of the man and citizen to walk in the path that was made clear to him, rather than in the way that was the light of others, was with him apparently a controlling maxim.

But it has appeared to me that, more than his aggressive and independent courage in affairs, religious and secular, more than his gift of that real eloquence which combines logic and sentiment in due and persuasive proportion, was his greatness shown in the all too-rare quality of cheerful and enduring fortitude in adversity. The systematic and organized assaults upon his personal character by enemies, and the still more trying estrangement of long-cherished friends, could not move him from the calm and even tenor of his way as a Christian teacher and a Christian man. In such an evil time he must have believed

> "That it becomes no man to nurse despair,
> But in the teeth of clenched antagonisms
> To follow up the worthiest till he die."

GEORGE F. EDMUNDS.

Washington.

THE PRESIDENT OF THE UNITED STATES.

WHILE I am by no means certain that anything I might prepare for the proposed memorial to the late Henry Ward Beecher would be worthy of a place among the eloquent and beautiful tributes which are sure to be presented, the request to furnish a contribution spurs to action my desire and intention to express to Mrs. Beecher more fully than I have yet done my sympathy in her affliction, and my appreciation of my own and the country's loss in the death of the great preacher.

More than thirty years ago I repeatedly enjoyed the opportunity of hearing him in his own pulpit. His warm utterances, and the earnest interest he displayed in the practical things related to useful living, the hopes he inspired, and the manner in which he relieved the precepts of Christianity from gloom and cheerlessness, made me feel that, though a stranger, he was my friend. Many years afterward we came to know each other, and since that time my belief in his friendship, based upon acquaintance and personal contact, has been to me a source of the greatest satisfaction.

His goodness and kindness of heart, so far as they were manifested in his personal life and in his home, are sacred to his family and to their grief; but, so far as they gave color and direction to his teachings and opinions, they are proper subjects for gratitude and congratulation on the part of every American citizen. They caused him to take the side of the common people in every discussion. He loved his fellows in their homes; he rejoiced in their contentment and comfort, and sympathized with them in their daily hardships and trials. As their champion, he advocated in all things the utmost regulated and wholesome liberty and freedom. His sublime faith in the success of popular government led him to trust the people, and to treat their errors and misconceptions with generous toleration. An honorable pride in American citizenship, guided by the teachings of religion, he believed to be a sure guaranty of a splendid national destiny. I never met Mr. Beecher without gaining something from his broad views and wise reflections.

The personal affliction of his family in his death stands alone in its magnitude and depth. But thousands wish that their sense of loss might temper the grief of that household, and that they, by sharing such sorrow, might lighten it. Such kindly assurances, and the realization of those who were knit to him by family ties, of the high and sacred mission accomplished in his useful life, furnish all this world can supply of comfort; but their faith and piety will not fail to lead them to a higher and better source of consolation.

GROVER CLEVELAND.

Washington.

ROBERT G. INGERSOLL.

HENRY WARD BEECHER was born in a Puritan penitentiary, of which his father was one of the wardens — a prison with very narrow and closely grated windows. Under its walls were the rayless, hopeless, and measureless dungeons of the damned, and on its roof fell the shadow of God's eternal frown. In this prison the creed and catechism were primers for children, and from a pure sense of duty their loving hearts were stained and scarred with the religion of John Calvin.

In those days the home of an orthodox minister was an inquisition in which babes were tortured for the good of their souls. Children then, as now, rebelled against the infamous absurdities and cruelties of the creed. No Calvinist was ever able, unless with blows, to answer the questions of his child. Children were raised in what was called " the nurture and admonition of the Lord,"—that is to say, their wills were broken or subdued, their natures deformed and dwarfed, their desires defeated or destroyed, and their development arrested or perverted. Life was robbed of its Spring, its Summer, and its Autumn. Children stepped from the cradle into the snow. No laughter, no sunshine, no joyous, free, unburdened days. God, an infinite detective, watched them from above, and Satan, with malicious leer, was waiting for their souls below. Between these monsters life was passed. Infinite consequences were predicated of the smallest action, and a burden greater than a god could bear was placed upon the heart and brain of every child. To think, to ask questions, to doubt, to investigate, were acts of rebellion. To express pity for the lost, writhing in the dungeons below, was simply to give evidence that the enemy of souls had been at work within their hearts.

Among all the religions of this world — from the creed of Cannibals who devoured flesh to that of Calvinists who polluted souls — there is none, there has been none, there will be none more utterly heartless and inhuman than was the orthodox Congregationalism of New England in the year of grace 1813. It despised every natural joy, hated pictures, abhorred statues as lewd and lustful things, execrated music, regarded Nature as fallen and corrupt, man as totally depraved, and woman as somewhat worse. The theater was the vestibule of perdition, actors the servants of Satan, and Shakespeare a trifling wretch, whose words were seeds of death. And yet the virtues found a welcome, cordial and sincere : duty was done as understood; obligations were discharged ; truth was told ; self-denial was practiced for the sake of others, and hearts were good and true in spite of book and creed.

In this atmosphere of theological miasma, in this hideous dream of superstition, in this penitentiary, moral and austere, this babe first saw the imprisoned gloom.

The natural desires ungratified, the laughter suppressed, the logic brow-beaten by authority, the humor frozen by fear,—of many generations,— were in this child — a child destined to rend and wreck the prison's walls.

Through the grated windows of his cell this child, this boy, this man caught glimpses of the outer world, of fields and skies. New thoughts were in his brain, new hopes within his heart. Another heaven bent above his life. There came a revelation of the beautiful and real. Theology grew mean and small.

Nature wooed, and won, and saved this mighty soul.

Her countless hands were sowing seeds within his tropic brain. All sights and sounds —all colors, forms, and fragments were stored within the treasury of his mind. His thoughts were molded by the graceful curves of streams, by winding paths in woods, the charm of quiet country roads and lanes grown indistinct with weeds and grass — by vines that cling and hide with leaf and flower the crumbling wall's decay — by cattle standing in the Summer pools like statues of content.

There was within his words the subtle spirit of the season's change — of everything that is, of everything that lies between the slumbering seeds, that half awakened by the April rain have dreams of heaven's blue and feel the amorous kisses of the sun, and that strange tomb wherein the Alchemist doth give to death's cold dust the throb and thrill of life again.

He saw with loving eyes the willows of the meadow-streams grow red beneath the glance of Spring — the grass along the marsh's edge — the stir of life beneath the withered leaves — the moss below the drip of snow — the flowers that give their bosoms to the first South wind that wooes — the sad and timid violets that only bear the gaze of love from eyes half closed — the ferns, where fancy gives a thousand forms with but a single plan — the green and sunny slopes enriched with daisy's silver and the cowslip's gold.

As in the leafless woods some tree aflame with life stands like a rapt poet in the heedless crowd, so stood this man among his fellow-men.

All there is of leaf and bud, of flower and fruit, of painted insect life, and all the winged and happy children of the air that Summer holds beneath her dome of blue, were known and loved by him.

He loved the yellow Autumn fields, the golden stacks, the happy homes of men, the orchard's bending boughs, the sumach's flags of flame, the maples with transfigured leaves, the tender yellow of the beech, the wondrous harmonies of brown and gold — the vines where hang the clustered spheres of wit and mirth. He loved the winter days, the whirl and drift of snow,— all forms of frost.— the rage and fury of the storm, when in the forest desolate and stripped the brave old pine towers green and grand — a prophesy of Spring. He heard the rhythmic sound of Nature's busy strife, the hum of bees, the songs of birds, the eagle's cry, the murmur of the streams, the sighs and lamentations of the winds and all the voices of the sea. He loved the shores, the vales, the crags and cliffs — the city's busy streets, the introspective, silent plain, the solemn splendors of the night, the silver sea of dawn and evening's clouds of molten gold.

The love of Nature freed this loving man.

One by one the fetters fell ; the gratings disappeared, the sunshine smote the roof, and on the floors of stone light streamed from open doors. He realized the darkness and despair, the cruelty and hate, the starless blackness of the old malignant creed. The flower of pity grew and blossomed in his heart. The selfish "consolation" filled his eyes with tears. He saw that what is called the Christian's hope is, that among the countless billions wrecked and lost, a meager few perhaps may reach the eternal shore — a hope that like the desert rain gives neither leaf nor bud — a hope that gives no joy, no peace, to any great and loving soul. It is the dust on which the serpent feeds that coils in heartless breasts.

Day by day the wrath and vengeance faded from the sky — the Jewish God grew vague and dim — the threats of torture and eternal pain grew vulgar and absurd, and all the miracles seemed strangely out of place. They clad the Infinite in motley garb, and gave to aureoled heads the cap and bells.

Touched by the pathos of all human life, knowing the shadows that fall on every heart, — the thorns in every path, the sighs, the sorrows, and the tears that lie between a mother's arms and death's embrace, — this great and gifted man denounced, denied, and damned with all his heart the fanged and frightful dogma that souls were made to feed the eternal hunger — ravenous as famine — of a God's revenge.

Take out this fearful, fiendish, heartless lie, — compared with which all other lies are true, — and the great arch of orthodox religion, crumbling, falls.

To the average man the Christian hell and heaven are only words. He has no scope of thought. He lives but in a dim, impoverished now. To him the past is dead — the future still unborn. He occupies with downcast eyes that narrow line of barren, shifting sand that lies between the flowing seas. But Genius knows all time. For him the dead all live and breathe and act their countless parts again. All human life is in his now, and every moment feels the thrill of all to be.

No one can overestimate the good accomplished by this marvelous, many-sided man. He helped to slay the heart-devouring monster of the Christian world. He tried to civilize the Church, to humanize the creeds. to soften pious breasts of stone. to take the fear from mother's hearts. the chains of creed from every brain, to put the star of hope in every sky and over every grave.

Attacked on every side, maligned by those who preached the law of love. he wavered not. but fought whole-hearted to the end.

Obstruction is but virtue's foil. From thwarted light leaps color's flame — the stream impeded has a song.

He passed from harsh and cruel creeds to that serene philosophy that has no place for pride or hate, that threatens no revenge, that looks on sin as stumblings of the blind, and pities those who fall, knowing that in the souls of all there is a sacred yearning for the light. He ceased to think of man as something thrust upon the world — an exile from some other sphere. He felt at last that men are part of Nature's self,—kindred of all life,—the gradual growth of countless years ; that all the sacred books were helps until outgrown, and all religions, rough and devious paths that man has worn with weary feet in sad and painful search for truth and peace. To him these paths were wrong. and yet all gave the promise of success. He knew that all the streams. no matter how they wander. turn, and curve amid the hills and rocks, or linger in the lakes and pools, must some time reach the sea.

These views enlarged his soul and made him patient with the world, and while the wintry snows of age were falling on his head, Spring. with all her wealth of bloom, was in his heart.

The memory of this ample man is now a part of Nature's wealth. He battled for the rights of men. His heart was with the slave. He stood against the selfish greed of millions banded to protect the pirate's trade. His voice was for the right when Freedom's friends were few. He taught the Church to think and doubt. He did not fear to stand alone. His brain took counsel of his heart. To every foe he offered reconciliation's hand. He loved this land of ours, and added to its glory through the world. He was the greatest orator that stood within the pulpit's narrow curve. He loved the liberty of speech. There was no trace of bigot in his blood. He was a brave and generous man, and so. with reverent hands, I place this tribute on his tomb.

ROBERT G. INGERSOLL.

New York City.

MR. GEORGE W. CABLE.

THE breadth of Henry Ward Beecher's generous nature reached over the differences between himself and other men and made it easy for him to draw near in spirit to every one to whom he drew near in the body. He found it no effort to enter into sympathy and helpful counsel with the highest and the lowest,— nay, the very highest and very lowest.

Several times I have lived day after day under the same roof with him. Every moment I have ever spent with him seems to me still one of special privilege. He united larger proportions of strength and benevolence than any other man I ever knew. He had a buoyant mirth, a pure love of play that rarely stays with men after they leave boyhood behind : but his was as fresh and abundant and pure at seventy-three as one could wish to see in a youth of eighteen.

Many will testify to the openness of his nature. The windows of his inner counsels seemed always standing wide open. It has never seemed to me credible that he could keep a secret of his own. Some men cannot bear the constraint of a buttoned and tied throat ; they must have air, air — down into their very bosoms. That seemed to me to be true of him in his moral nature. As far as he could take thought of himself, he was careful for one thing—his character; reputation was another. He seemed to come nearer counting it mere dross than — even than men ought to.

He seemed to live by moral courage. He loved to feel himself put to proof. He loved warfare, if only the weapons were the weapons of peace and love and he could be on the side he believed in as the line of right and of mercy. He loved the strife that makes for better peace and deeper love. The result was he never had to spare the faults of any person or community lest he should "lose his influence" there. Love was his motive, his influence, and the impulse to which he appealed. The power of his religious teachings was—among other things of which many will speak—a degree of condescension that was almost condescension without degree. Nearer than any other preacher within my limited knowledge, he imposed no conditions of salvation upon sinning men and women save what Christ would have imposed had the Master stood in his footprints. He said to me once, "I have taken *atheists* into

my Sabbath-school and put them to teaching friendless boys such
things of Scripture as they could honestly vouch for; and some
such are to-day among the truest and most fruitful Christians in
my church."

We cannot truly call the departure of such men from the earth a
loss to the world. When the fruit is ripe, let it be picked. A man
of worth who has filled out the span of human life never can attain
his greatest worth or might except by dying. "Except the corn
of wheat fall into the ground, it abideth alone." The world will
gather more fruit and gather it the sooner because that great tree
lies felled with all its laden branches pouring their fruitage out upon
the sod. "He—all the more—being dead, yet speaketh."

GEORGE W. CABLE.

Northampton, Mass.

THE REV. PROFESSOR DAVID SWING.

IN looking over the great career of Henry Ward Beecher, the
greatest years of his wonderful life were, in my opinion, those
lying between 1845 and 1865. That group of twenty years was
made tremendous by the great ideas which lay beneath them.
These great years would have been thirty, had not his large themes
died from fulfillment. His mind and body were equal to a longer
service, but England needed no longer any instruction as to America;
Kansas needed no more intercession; the slaves needed no more
of the eloquence of abolition. The cathedral of liberty had been
completed, and the architect had only to go inside and become a
worshiper. For twenty years this wonderful man worked for the
human race, then he wrought twenty more years for his parish,
this last score of summers being also full of power, but not to be
compared with the time when the toil was for the nation, and the
tasks the greatest upon earth. In the greater period he seemed
under the employ of the people to plead their cause in politics and
religion. His pulpit moved around in the daily press, and was on
the banks of the Ohio and the Missouri, while, as the old Scottish

clans sprang forth from the bushes when their chieftain gave a blast
on his trumpet, the audiences of this evangelist issued at his
call from all the hills of the East and the waving grass of the West.
The public services of Daniel Webster did not cover so wide a space
of time, nor did the great career of Abraham Lincoln take in so
many circles of the sun; to Henry Ward Beecher must be given the
fame and gratitude for a battle long fought, and well fought to
the final perfect triumph. He performed a tremendous work, and
now, when his grave is made in a nation which is a unit, a nation
dedicated indeed to liberty, a nation whose South is pressing on
toward industry, wealth, education ; a republic whose name is now
respected by every throne and every cottage throughout the civilized
world,—that grave ought to catch from the whole country its
mingled flowers and its tears.

DAVID SWING.

Chicago.

MISS EMMA ABBOTT.

THE whole civilized world mourns the great loss suffered in the
death of Henry Ward Beecher, and thousands of hearts are
aching at the departure of one whose noble soul was filled with love
and charity for all mankind, and whose humanity was as broad and
glorious and far-reaching as the blessed sunshine. How his words
of comfort have sustained those whose burdens seemed greater
than they could bear, how many thousands of erring ones he has
turned from the paths of evil, and how many sorrowing hearts he
has comforted, the good Father, who loves us all, knows, and will
reward.

Henry Ward Beecher was the greatest preacher of the Gospel
since the days of Paul, and like Paul when nearing the shadow of
the grave, he could give this testimony with a full heart : "For me
to live is Christ, and to die is gain."

EMMA ABBOTT.

Pittsburgh.

HENRY WARD BEECHER.

A MEMORY OF A SERMON.

OUT of the past comes forth one Sabbath-day,
  A silvering head uplifted from the crowd
That the great preacher's eloquence could sway
  Like wind-swept wheat : a voice not low nor loud.

Varying from gentle to impetuous force
  As changeful inspirations struck the keys
Of utterance : like a torrent in its course,
  Breaking apart into new harmonies.

Unspoken thoughts rose. struggling underneath
  The current of expression. deepening still
The emphasis of full and steady breath
  That, poised in silence, seemed the house to fill.

Slow came the words, as when swift waters lie
  Calmed in the pool whereunto they have run :
" Brethren, this will I strive for till I die—
  Union in Christ. his sundered flock made one."

The voice is hushed ; the impulse that it gave
  Is moving onward like an army's tread :
The man who helped the outcast and the slave,
  And loved the little children. is not dead !

He lived in this great human family
  As in the all-embracing church of God.
He lives here still : a freer path have we
  Since with so free a step our earth he trod.

The petty shibboleths of sect and clan
  His lips refused. rejected to the end :
His manhood met itself in every man.
  He counted even his enemy his friend.

What grander glory to attain than this ?
  To be an overflow of God. a force

Magnetically fusing lives in his,
  The father of all spirits, our life's source.

There are men — he was one — whose atmosphere
  Breathes freshening vigor through earth's drowsy air:
The master in the servant so draws near,
  And hearts leap up His sacrifice to share.

The day is dawning; beautiful the glow
  Upon the mountains, of Christ's coming feet;
And the prophetic heavens already know
  His world redeemed, His church in Him complete,

The purpose this man lived for cannot die,
  The fire is kindled, and the work begun;
And still he urges, from the neighboring sky,
  "O brethren, in the name of Christ, be one!"

LUCY LARCOM.

Beverly, Mass.

MR. GEORGE W. CHILDS.

To the personal sorrow that the death of Henry Ward Beecher brought with it to friends on both sides of the Atlantic, there was added the loss of a gifted public censor on large affairs. It was not Mr. Beecher's practice to discuss such affairs from the sentimental side alone, and he seldom allowed fervor to usurp the office of facts. From his conclusions and his opinions hearers might often differ, but there was little room for doubt that he had studied the case by way of preparation. A large part of the preacher's influence over his hearers was due to his abounding physical health and his joyousness of nature. He presented nearly always a cheerful outlook; he trusted to common sense to decide questions of personal or public duty. This extended his influence widely over minds non-receptive to what is usually called preaching.

His renown was not built exclusively or even mostly upon his achievements as one of the very few supremely able pulpit orators of his day. On a par with his gift of rare eloquence were his sturdy and stalwart self-reliance and independence of character; his earnest and uncompromising patriotism; his universal sympathy for the suffering and oppressed; and his championship of the cause of liberty for all men, in all countries, under all circumstances. His repartees had a quality that enlightened as well as penetrated. They were arguments in a flash of lightning. He seemed, as a preacher, to put himself in the pews, rather than to lecture from the pulpit. He had some of the qualities that make the Methodist circuit-rider and the Catholic missionary powers in their offices, and had no more air of condescension as from man to man than Abraham Lincoln had. Like Lincoln, he stood on many occasions for incarnate common sense.

GEORGE W. CHILDS.

Philadelphia.

HON. ALONZO B. CORNELL.

FOR forty years Henry Ward Beecher commanded the respectful attention of the American people without becoming tiresome or unwelcome. In pulpit, press, and popular address, he made almost daily expression upon an endless variety of subjects, and was probably listened to by a larger number of persons than any other man of his generation. Frank, fearless, and eloquent in address, seldom an auditorium could accommodate the multitude seeking admission where he was announced to speak. Unrivaled as a preacher of the gospel; matchless as a popular orator; tireless as a champion of human rights; versatile in knowledge; profound in thought, and of the broadest liberality in his views, he exerted a powerful influence in advancing the intelligence and elevating the morality of mankind. His life-work, fairly considered, constitutes a record of intellectual activity and achievement quite unprecedented in our history.

ALONZO B. CORNELL.

New York City.

GENERAL J. M. SCHOFIELD.

Not being so fortunate as to have known Mr. Beecher personally, yet his personality seemed for many years nearly as familiar to me as that of any one with whom I have been closely associated. I have long esteemed him as one of the very greatest men of the age. In him great intellectual endowment was most happily united with nobleness of soul, the most ardent patriotism with the broadest philanthropy, and the most exalted religious faith with Christian love and charity superior to all creeds and yearning to embrace all mankind. Mr. Beecher's memory must ever be dear to all patriotic Americans, and especially to every Union soldier, and I gladly pay my humble tribute of reverence and respect to the memory of so great and good a fellow-citizen.

J. M. SCHOFIELD.

Governor's Island, New York Harbor.

MR. DION BOUCICAULT.

It was in the editorial rooms of the New York "Tribune," just thirty years ago, that I first met Henry Ward Beecher. It was either Charles A. Dana or Horace Greeley that made us known to each other. We had appeared as antagonists in the columns of that journal, Mr. Beecher attacking the stage and I defending it. One phrase in my article seemed to amuse him; it was where it was urged that "there was more crime and debauchery committed on a Sunday than on any other day of the week, but let us not be uncharitable enough to believe that this fact is attributable to the churches being open on that day, and the theaters shut." Mr. Beecher remarked that this kind of sparring was "hitting under the belt." We spoke at length, and I found that he held very deeply rooted opinions on this subject.

Three years ago, we met again in Denver. To my surprise, he recalled our interview of 1857, and our little battle in the columns of the "Tribune." With a frankness that was the principal charm of his grand self, he told me he had learned amongst other truths how wrong he was in the prejudice he had entertained against the stage. "There is," said he, "good and evil in everything, and it is the mission of the Christian to cultivate the good and root out the evil." He went on to enumerate the number of great men from Sophocles to Shakespeare, nobles of the human race, that had been the children of the drama. I remarked that many sincere and good people objected to the stage because its very soul was a fiction, and its art was a moral conveyed in a falsehood. After a reflection of a moment, he remarked, almost to himself, "And the parables of our Saviour?"

Beecher fills a grave. But no man can fill the grave that he has left in the world above the sod and under the sun. "He was a man, take him for all in all. We shall not look upon his like again."

DION BOUCICAULT.

New York City.

MR. NOAH BROOKS.

OF Henry Ward Beecher it may be truly said that he touched nothing that he did not ornament. His was a comprehensive and all-embracing mind. There was nothing too vast to discourage his adventurous curiosity, nothing too small to engage his earnest attention. Everything that touched humanity at any point was of interest to him. And upon all of these things he poured the light of one of the most richly endowed minds ever given to man. His career stretched over some of the most momentous events in our history as a nation. He saw the peopling of the New West, the building of great cities, the rise of the slave power, the growth of the spirit of human liberty, the slaveholder's rebellion, the downfall of the accursed institution, the restoration of honorable peace and the rehabilitation of the New South. In all these mighty matters he had some share; and in many of them he put forth a giant's strength to the pulling down of the strongholds of wrong and crime. And, through all these years, often tense with portentous events, how zealously he has filled the measure of his days with the innumerable cares of pastor, friend, husband, father, neighbor, and citizen, it is impossible to describe.

It cannot be hoped for any human being that he shall be able by industry, self-denial, study, research, or training to be a Beecher. His genius was God-given. He was one of those rare men of whom we have few examples in the history of the race. Generations may pass before another worthy of an intimate comparison to him shall appear upon the earth.

NOAH BROOKS.

Newark, New Jersey.

M. DOCTOR LOUIS PASTEUR.

WERE it not for my health, which for some months past has been, and is still, so very poor, I would feel myself impelled to send you a final tribute of respect to the late Rev. Henry Ward Beecher.

Prevented by illness to do this, I should like at least to express to the widow and to the family of this noble man the sympathy that I feel in their sorrow,—a sorrow shared by humanity everywhere.

L. PASTEUR.

Arbois (Jura), France.

REV. THEODORE L. CUYLER, D. D.

DURING the most brilliant period of Mr. Beecher's marvelous career I was associated very intimately with him on the platform and in various reformatory movements. I knew him thoroughly, I loved him intensely. Among the great galaxy of the champions of freedom which embraced Sumner, Chase, Garrison, Phillips, and Whittier, the star which hung over Brooklyn Heights rode resplendent. It was a guiding star to many a refugee from the house of bondage. The generation of Americans now coming on the stage can scarcely comprehend what a degree of unflinching

courage it required to be a champion of freedom forty years ago.
But Beecher never grew purple in the lips. That Harry Percy of
liberty never showed the white feather or turned his back. Of his
marvelous charms of eloquence I need no more write than of the
grandeur of Handel's oratorios. It was something to dream about.
His voice was as sweet as a lute, and as loud as a trumpet. In its
tenderest pathos, that witching voice touched the fount of tears.
When he rose into impassioned sublimity " they that heard him said
that it thundered." And now that the marvelous voice is stilled
in death, we will all confess that we shall not hear its like again.

Henry Ward Beecher's place in American history is sure. As an
orator he will take rank with Whitefield, Patrick Henry, and Phillips.
As the champion of human rights his proud place will be beside
John Quincy Adams and Charles Sumner. And in the hearts of
the negro freedmen the name of Beecher will nestle alongside of
that of Abraham Lincoln.

THEODORE L. CUYLER.

Brooklyn.

MRS. SARA J. LIPPINCOTT. (Grace Greenwood.)

To me the death of Henry Ward Beecher, an event so infinitely
sad to those who knew him intimately, has brought a profound dejection, a strange sense of discouragement and impover-
ishment, which increases in heaviness day by day ; for, perhaps
from being so far away from my country, I had difficulty at first
in realizing her loss as an absolute inexorable fact. I had not met
Mr. Beecher of late years. I never had the honor of a familiar personal acquaintance with him, and this feeling of depression and
deprivation would seem scarcely natural, were it not that for me,
who am inclined to take rather a mournful and morbid view of life, to
rebel against the inevitable and inscrutable, and to see if there is
not more evil than good, more suffering than happiness among all
God's creatures, this wonderful many-sided man has always been
the ideal and embodiment of courageous cheerfulness, and uncon-

sciously I was helped by him while he lived his strong, cheery life on earth. Such a life is a tonic for all the world. Mr. Beecher was an optimist from a happy organization, and a philosopher from principle. To him nature revealed her utmost brightness and lightness, for him God smiled through his most darksome providences. He was the prophet of good cheer. He foretold " a good time coming" for the most unfortunate of his fellow-men, but he took his good time out of the days as they passed. He must have suffered some fierce and fiery onslaughts from the demons of doubt, discouragement, and despondency, but he never surrendered. He kept his good spirits up by work, and his work by good spirits. He did not, Luther-like, fling his inkstand at the devil, only his ink,—making the tempter blacker and uglier than ever. I have always had especial need of such sunny, yet bracing and breezy moral and intellectual influence as he exerted. I remember that in the old days, when I passed out from Plymouth Church, the sun was always shining for me whatever the weather, and that I found my heart had been lightened of some burden of care, regret, or dread, by a lift of brotherly sympathy, by a few tears shed for the woes or wrongs of others, or by a little hearty, healthful laughter, which *had* to come.

So I leave to other friends and admirers of the great preacher to pay tributes to his genius, his broad humanity, his matchless oratory, his patriotism and piety, while I offer mine to that quality more rare than eloquence, more heroic than heroism, more sweet and serving than much which is called religion,—his simple, manly, steadfast cheerfulness. Let other hands bring to his grave laurels for his greatness, rich, red. deep-hearted roses for his humanity, costly and fragrant exotics as emblems of his rare poetic gifts and brilliant social qualities, but let me lay thereon, as types of that hopeful, helpful characteristic which I so admired and coveted, a simple bunch of spring-flowers, from the woods and fields,—the brave arbutus, thrusting aside the dry leaves of a dead past and daring keen winds and biting frosts; the primrose, laughing up from the yet brown turf; tiny buttercups and daisies; and even that small prophet of the sun, the golden dandelion,—common brighteners of our common ways, which we walk among with lightened steps, not knowing what cheers us.

For his people, the going hence of their great friend means so much gone out of life which helped them to bear life, under its hardest and saddest conditions, that they cannot in their human weakness rejoice for him who will rejoice them no more. It will long be hard for them even to smile over recollections of his pleasant jests and quaint sayings, for thinking that the voice that uttered them is silent forever, and that the face once illumined by the flash of wit and the glow of happy fancies is hid away from them in deep stillness and ever-during night.

GRACE GREENWOOD.

Milan, Italy.

HON. SAMUEL S. COX.

I OFTEN heard Henry Ward Beecher upon the platform, and not infrequently in the pulpit. From certain peculiar relations to him, or those who are near to him, I have had occasion to know him personally. Aside from his social magnetism, which drew so many friends around him, aside from the quick susceptibility which he had in all matters of taste, I think the capital element in his nature, as developed in his sermons, as well as in his lectures, was a large, roundabout, homely way of saying things which attracted the general attention and left an indelible impression. To produce this impression I noticed that he, like others of his family, including his father, whom I knew, drew his similes from the domestic relations,—from the hearth, from all home life and those associations connected with children and parents, brothers and sisters. There was a simplicity and directness about these illustrations that gave force to the idea conveyed.

In dealing with matters connected with our own country of which I have been observant, and especially since the war, when the generosities of our nature were most called into vogue, he never failed to take the liberal side. I remember once when Mr. Beecher was on a lecturing visit to Washington, a bill was pending for the payment to an old captain in the navy of a small sum which had been found due to him in his accounts. A leader in the House violently attacked the bill because the old naval officer, when the war broke out, had sided with his State, although too old to take any active part as a belligerent. This bill led to quite an acrimonious debate, in which nearly all the passions of the war were involved, and all the generosities connected with our better feeling toward those who were reinstated in our councils were also involved. I took some part in the debate, and noticed that I had very earnest applause from a gentleman seated all alone in the diplomatic gallery. On looking round, I recognized Henry Ward Beecher! This is but one illustration of a thousand of the liberality of his nature; and it is well to understand, when speaking of his public services as an index of his character, that there was not one attribute. so far as my observation went, looking to retaliation or resentment toward those of the South who had been in arms against the Government.

His rhetorical powers to me were remarkable, and he could sway men and women and hold them in a spell of enchantment with wonderful power. I could not see that to the end of his life he had failed in any effort in "gracing the noble fervor of an hour" by words instinct with great deeds.

S. S. COX.

Washington.

PROFESSOR ALEXANDER GRAHAM BELL.

I HAVE no special claim to justify a contribution to this memorial volume in honor of Henry Ward Beecher beyond that of being a sincere admirer of his spirit and work. All who ever heard Mr. Beecher, as well as the larger number who are only familiar with his achievements, cannot but revere the memory of so great a spokesman of patriotism and humanity. His death is a loss to the age, for his influence extended throughout the Old World and the New; and I cannot wish better for our future than that the example set by Mr. Beecher of bravery, honesty, public spirit, and geniality may be widely emulated. He bequeathed to us a mold of greatness in his record.

ALEXANDER GRAHAM BELL.

Washington.

HON. DAVID DUDLEY FIELD.

To me, Henry Ward Beecher was at once a great preacher, lecturer, and author. His sermons were unlike any other that I ever heard, always full of thought, often eloquent, and sometimes sparkling with a quiet humor which quickened the attention of his hearers. His lectures were a mixture of wit and eloquence, and when, as at the time of the antislavery agitation and the civil war, he was greatly in earnest, his sentences ground to powder the arguments of his adversaries. His books will always keep their place in the library. Mr. Beecher's influence has been great upon his generation. He spoke from more pulpits and platforms than any other man of his time, and the good that he did can hardly be measured.

DAVID DUDLEY FIELD.

New York City.

HON. MURAT HALSTEAD.

From Mr. Beecher's life the young men of the day can learn a most valuable lesson,—that of his enthusiastic and persevering industry. The amount of labor that he performed was prodigious, and he did not flinch, from his boyhood until the day when he was stricken by the wing of the angel of death; and he never toiled with greater assiduity and intensity than through the last weeks of his life in writing the second and unfinished volume of his "Life of Christ." I may here recite the lines of Longfellow on the death of Hawthorne:

> "Who shall lift the wand of magic power,
>   The lost clew regain?
> The unfinished window in Aladdin's tower
>   Unfinished must remain."

Mr. Beecher was not born to rest in this world, but to strive always. He was like the blooded horse that is carried on by his inherent fire, which forbids lash or spur, but runs the race to the end,—the race that endures until the immortal spark passes to its brighter part in the inextinguishable illumination. He was one of the master workingmen of the world, and has entered into rest.

His death leaves a great gap in the ranks of the men of mark on the horizon of the world, like that made by the fall of one of the grand old trees through whose lofty head we have been accustomed to behold the glories of the skies, and that seemed firm and familiar as the hills.

MURAT HALSTEAD.

Cincinnati.

REV. NEWMAN HALL, D. D., LL. D.

MY sorrowful and strong disapproval of some of Mr. Beecher's theological utterances in later years in no degree lessens my admiration of his genius, his unrivaled eloquence, and his labors as a philanthropist. He has been a link of brotherhood between New and Old England, and has left an indelible mark on the history of his own country. His life-long vindication of the rights of humanity, and especially his persistent advocacy of freedom for the colored race, when such advocacy was generally denounced, entitle him to the high plane he has won among the benefactors of mankind.

NEWMAN HALL.

London.

GENERAL WILLIAM S. ROSECRANS.

THE patriotic enthusiasm for our country, the vigor, eloquence, and effectiveness with which Henry Ward Beecher spoke and wrote for the Union made us kin. It has seemed to me that a noble hatred of wrong and injustice always vigorously moved his impetuous nature, and yet but rarely so that pretended victims secured his services for the undeserving. His thoughts seemed to lift the imagination toward a higher and better life, while his energetic, active life moved people to become better citizens, better neighbors, and better men and women. In a life of rare usefulness and public prominence, he set a noble example of speaking and acting on his convictions in an age and country when men who have the courage of their convictions are always needed and none too numerous.

W. S. ROSECRANS.

Washington.

REV. WILLIAM ORMISTON, D. D., LL. D.

For many years I regularly read the published sermons of Henry Ward Beecher, long before I ever had the pleasure of meeting him personally, and I was struck with the wondrous power and versatility of the preacher. Notwithstanding the fact that his theology did not always agree with mine, I was ever mentally stimulated and greatly instructed by his eloquent address. His productions had a peculiar charm and exercised a great power over me.

In 1870, I came to New York and received a characteristic warm welcome from Mr. Beecher, and I was delighted with my personal intercourse with him. I was perfectly charmed by his frank and genial manners, and greatly admired him. I am glad that I knew him. I seldom heard him preach, but had the privilege of frequently listening to his public lectures and addresses, many of which were masterpieces of forensic and persuasive eloquence, and roused his audience to the highest pitch of lofty enthusiasm. As an orator on public occasions, I deem him without a rival. Others may have excelled him in some aspects, but, as a speaker, with a resistless magnetism to control and move great masses of people on any philanthropic or patriotic theme, he was unsurpassed.

He has, in my judgment, left no man in America to-day of equal potency as a speaker, or who can so touch the hearts of an American audience, or so effectively present the position and claims of the United States to an English assembly as he did a few years ago. He was a man of strong and fearless convictions, of dauntless and heroic courage, of broad and boundless charity,—a man to be greatly beloved while living, and fondly remembered when dead. His name will be placed high on the list of the nation's most gifted and honored sons, and it may be fitly said of him what Antony said of Brutus:

> "His life was gentle ; and the elements
> So mixed in him, that nature might stand up
> And say to all the world, 'This was a man.'

W. ORMISTON.

New York City.

DR. GEORGE H. HEPWORTH.

THE magnificent gifts which characterized Henry Ward Beecher as a platform speaker, and his rare power in the pulpit, are themes which every man in the country can talk about. Of all the throngs which every year pour into New York from every section of the Union, for pleasure or business, hardly a man thought he had finished his work well until he had been to hear Beecher, and had noted down in his memory some quaint saying or incident for recital on his return home. He was phenomenal in his ability to make people love him. He was by nature so kindly, so genuinely generous, that he took you captive at the very start. And although he was conscious of his vast influence over the minds and hearts of the people, he somehow never acquired a lofty manner of condescension when he spoke to ordinary folk, but was as familiar as though your brains and his were made out of the same sort of stuff, though both of you knew well enough that they were not. The truth is, he preached his greatest sermons so easily that he hardly knew himself how he did it; and while he felt gratified at what had been done, he was oftentimes humbled in the midst of his triumph by a depressing fear that he would never again be able to equal that accomplishment. All this signifies that Henry Ward Beecher was a genius, with the peculiarities of temperament which the word suggests.

GEORGE H. HEPWORTH.

New York City.

4

MR. W. W. CORCORAN.

NEVER having had the advantage of meeting Mr. Beecher, or of proving by my personal experience the extraordinary power he possessed as a pulpit and platform orator, I cannot properly offer any testimony of my own in the hope of adding evidence to the esteem in which he was held by his friends, or of swelling the applause which waited on him at the hands of the people whose hearts he touched, and whose opinions he swayed. Gifted as he was with a faculty of public utterance by which he often caused his words to echo throughout the whole land, no testimony to his commanding powers of mind and of popular oratory can be so strong as that which may be found in the wild enthusiasm he excited and the strong antagonisms he sometimes provoked.

That his last days were spent in the cause of civic reconciliation and of national fraternity, should be a source of congratulation to all his countrymen.

W. W. CORCORAN.

Washington.

HON. J. B. GRINNELL.

WITHOUT military exploits or official civil service, Henry Ward Beecher was daring in confronting public opinion with matchless speech, unique personality, and rigid example. Alone he stands as the American divine, who chose to make his place rather than fill one made, and gathered and held for forty years the largest Christian congregation ever convened on this continent. He was an artist, dexterous in the use of the moralist's weapons, supreme in separating dross from gold in the fiery alembics of a soul impatient with device or neutrality. He was indeed a bold patriot, an ardent lover, a humble Christian, and a princely preacher. For years he molded my thoughts more than did any other man of the present time, and I am proud to offer this humble tribute to his memory.

J. B. GRINNELL.

Grinnell, Iowa.

HON. ROSCOE CONKLING.

To assert the genius, the remarkable powers, or the fame of Henry Ward Beecher is as needless for this generation as to certify the light of the sun. The diversity of his gifts and acquirements enabled him to appear with distinction before vast numbers of his fellow-men in more varied fields than perhaps any other man of his time. As orator, writer, preacher, philanthropist, and leader of sentiment, his position was so conspicuous, so almost solitary, and universally known that testimony is silenced by the consciousness that it is so needless. His own words are not mute, nor will they be mute as long as anything we say of him is remembered.

ROSCOE CONKLING.

New York City.

MRS. J. C. CROLY ("JENNY JUNE").

MR. BEECHER was, perhaps, the greatest man that has lived in this century: the broadest, most human, most sympathetic, most comprehensive in his recognition of excellencies and toleration of men's ideas and opinions. The strength of his feelings alone prevented him from putting the finest finishing-touch of art upon his magnificent oratory; but this instant and intense responsiveness added greatly to his power as a leader, and gave it that strength of personal influence which no attacks could weaken. No worthy cause wanted a champion while he lived, no individual could be honored if Henry Ward Beecher was absent. His mighty congregation was drawn from the ends of the earth, and the open doors of his church were maintained with loving liberality by its members, whom he educated to this spirit of fellowship with the whole human race. There will be other great preachers and other great men, but it will be long before preacher and man are united in another Henry Ward Beecher.

JENNY JUNE.

New York City

HON. PRESTON B. PLUMB,

UNITED STATES SENATOR FROM KANSAS.

THE people of Kansas share with all the English-speaking race in the admiration and respect which Mr. Beecher's talents and character inspired. The charm of his eloquence, the force and clearness of his demonstrations, the skill and power of his controversial essays, his patience and fortitude under trials,— these are qualities and attributes happily united in the character and career of the illustrious divine.

Perhaps even more conspicuous was the influence of his personality upon those with whom he was immediately associated. This was strikingly exhibited in the founding and phenomenal development of a religious institution, which, great as it is in the varied elements which dignify and strengthen human association, still derives its chief title to fame from his matchless leadership.

The people of Kansas have special reason for offering their tribute to the memory of Henry Ward Beecher. He was their friend when friends were sorely needed. When the future of that Commonwealth and the fate of Freedom itself trembled in the balance, no voice more eloquent or more influential than his was lifted in their behalf. He had the wisdom to recognize the gravity of the situation, and the boldness to advocate the only measures fitted to the time. He saw that the forcible encroachments of slavery could only be successfully resisted by force, and he assumed the responsibility of advising that the crisis be heroically met.

Nearly a third of a century has passed since that troubled period ended. Many of those who participated in its struggles and trials still inhabit the State born of so much commotion. They and their successors are not likely to forget the services, the sacrifices, and the offerings of those to whose patriotic exertions are due, in so large a degree, the peaceful triumphs of these later years. In that notable array the name of Henry Ward Beecher will not shine less brightly when time shall have still further softened the asperities of the past and still further multiplied the fruits of the establishment of freedom in Kansas.

P. B. PLUMB.

Washington.

HON. HAMILTON FISH.

IT was not my good fortune to have any familiar personal acquaintance with Mr. Beecher, but I have listened upon several occasions to public addresses delivered by him, and I need not say, always did so with admiration of his learning, his eloquence, and his fascinating influence upon his audience. His warm devotion to the Union, and his active and efficient labors in behalf of the nation during its struggle for existence, and his eloquent appeals in behalf of the freedom of the slave, will ever enshrine his name in the gratitude and admiration of future ages.

HAMILTON FISH.

New York City.

REV. EDWARD McGLYNN, D. D.

FOREMOST in the work of hastening the coming of the better day was the great man whose memory we perpetuate in these memorial pages. None others so well understood, as he taught the men of his land and time to exalt, the essentials of religion, pure and undefiled, in which we all agree, and to minimize the differences that seem to separate us. To him was given to see with clearer vision, to reveal with unequaled genius, and with tireless energy to make common among men the meaning of Him who taught of old on the mount and by the sea-shore the core of all religion — the fatherhood of God and the brotherhood of man. I cheerfully confess that from Mr. Beecher I learned, from the first days of my ministry, a new tenderness and fullness of meaning in the " Our Father," and I am glad to be able here to state that the theology of the old church agrees with his in this: that the essence of religion is in communion with God through the love of Him for His own sake, and in loving all men for God's sake with the best love with which we love ourselves, and that while sacrifice and sacrament, creed and ritual, prayer and sermon and song may be and are powerful helps and necessary manifestations of this religion, which is love, without it they are but a mockery, a sacrilege and a blasphemy.

EDWARD McGLYNN.

New York City.

MRS. LAURA C. HOLLOWAY.

H AD I not a recollection of gratitude for the welcome he gave to Southerners who, as exiles from home, had come to dwell among his friends, there would be no reason sufficient for me to write of Mr. Beecher, for there is not a tribute possible to offer his memory which has not been repeatedly bestowed.

His genius made him a many-sided man — and his fame is unequaled by that of any American of his day. Possessed of unerring intuition and a mental outlook which made him appear prophetic, he was abreast if not ahead of the advanced thinkers of the age. But so well he knew his kind that he held himself to the pace of those to whom he was ministering, and if perchance he momentarily traveled too fast for them, his humor and pathos were powerful aids to successful retreat from a too-advanced position. He never fought his way ahead of his followers, so as to estrange even the weakest about him, and the absolute influence he exercised over his congregation made even his most ultra views on public questions palatable to them.

Catholicity of spirit was the mighty force he exerted to draw men to him, and there was enough in his thought to supply all varieties of natures. He was, in the occult sense in which St. Paul meant it, "all things to all men." A Brahmin, a Parsee, a Buddhist, a Catholic or a Mohammedan could find points of agreement with him, and his largeness of nature made him a refuge for people of all diversities of belief. He constantly asserted the brotherhood of religions as well as the brotherhood of man, and no American preacher ever has had so many different representatives of humanity listen to him as had Mr. Beecher. Those who were not impressed by what he said were impressed with his manner of saying it. He was a broad, strong, and brilliant ray of sunshine in the world, whose blotting out has left a great and dark void in the hearts of men. When his personality has faded out of the public mind, or, rather, when generations have succeeded the ones which knew him, his memory will be preserved in a shrine on which will be inscribed, " He loved his fellow-men."

LAURA C. HOLLOWAY.

Brooklyn.

HON. CHARLES STEWART PARNELL, M. P.

In behalf of myself and my colleagues, I would convey an expression of profound sympathy at the death of Henry Ward Beecher. His name will ever remain dear to every Irishman, and all lovers of liberty and justice, as one of the noblest, bravest, and most gifted apostles of human rights.

CHARLES STEWART PARNELL.

London.

MR. HENRY GEORGE.

I am glad to express my respect for the memory of Henry Ward Beecher, and my deep appreciation of the good work he did.

Henry Ward Beecher encountered what in the nature of things must always be encountered by those who fight in the van of a struggle against a great wrong — ridicule, abuse, misrepresentation, and all but personal violence. Yet, as the good cause he espoused grew and strengthened, his influence grew with it, and even while he was yet probably the most abused and most hated man in the United States, he was pastor of the largest and strongest congregation in the whole country, and radiated from his pulpit an influence that reached the remotest corners of the earth. It was not because of his talents alone that Henry Ward Beecher was great and powerful, and that there came to him that highest of all rewards that can come to man — the reward of seeing his own efforts tell perceptibly in the advancement of a great cause. His preaching, ridiculed and denounced by the scribes and Pharisees of the time as the bringing of politics into religion, the mingling of secular with sacred things, had in it that power which enabled early Christianity to sweep over the Roman world and into barbarian lands — the arousing of the religious sentiment to work reform on earth.

And when at last the antislavery struggle burst into the consuming flame of civil war, it was given to Henry Ward Beecher, not only to animate the patriotism and devotion that maintained the

Union, but in a foreign land to perform a notable service to his country and to humanity. He lived to see the great cause with which his name had been identified fully triumphant; to see the fierce passions the strife had excited stilled to peace, to clasp in friendship the hands of those who had once been bitter enemies, and to exert in other directions an influence for good. Some lives are longer, but few are more full and useful than was his.

HENRY GEORGE.

New York City.

REV. LYMAN ABBOTT, D. D.

I⊤ would be idle for me to express a recognition, and impossible for me to attempt an analysis of Mr. Beecher's genius. To those who stood nearest to him and knew him best he was as good as he was great, or, to speak more accurately, as great in moral and spiritual qualities as in intellectual abilities. He was most Titanesque to those who knew him most intimately. Absolutely without self-conceit, yet on occasion possessed with a full consciousness of his power; without the weakness which excessive approbativeness always produces, yet with that quickness of sympathy which is rarely disassociated from approbativeness; with a universal perception of all the phenomena of nature, yet with a purity of soul and of life which we usually associate only with the innocence of ignorance; with great power of reserve, yet absolutely transparent, capable of silence, but incapable of deceit or falsehood; generous to a fault, and most generous to those who had the least claim upon his generosity, — the self-contradictions of his nature were those of a character wonderfully well balanced in moral equipoise. Great men have faults, but the faults of Mr. Beecher were defects, not vices. They lay in methods of expression, and sometimes of action, never in the spiritual purposes which dominated and controlled him; they were blemishes on the surface; they did not poison the sap and fiber of his being. The secret of all lay, as I believe, in his devout faith, in the predominance of his spiritual faculties in what the Bible calls godliness.

LYMAN ABBOTT

New York City.

HON. HANNIBAL HAMLIN.

I REGARDED the late Henry Ward Beecher as one of the most eminent divines of this age, if not of all time. He did a great and
good work in brushing away the cobwebs of time that clung around
the old schools of theology, and in advancing the intellectual, moral,
and social condition of mankind. And he did a grand work, as I
know, in preserving the life and unity of the nation during the late
rebellion. The great value of that work can only be comprehended
and appreciated by those who intimately understood it. For that
work his memory should be embalmed and cherished by all who
love our country and its free institutions.

HANNIBAL HAMLIN.

Bangor, Maine.

REV. MARK HOPKINS, D. D., LL. D.

SOON after Mr. Beecher was settled in Brooklyn he came to
Williams College to address the Adelphic Union Society. The
desire to hear him was even then so great that he was obliged to
enter the church by one of the windows. No one who heard him
was disappointed. After giving the address, he remained a day or
two for trout-fishing, and during the time was my guest. Few
men, I am sure, who have ever lived could have created, in so
short a time, so strong a personal interest. His spontaneity was
that of a fountain, and his sparkling and kindly talk was like the
glad rippling of water in the sunshine.

There was in him then, at or near its fullness, that combination
of playfulness with insight and power that gave him such a hold
on his friends. From that time I knew him only as the people
knew him, but never lost my strong personal regard. This led
me to rejoice in his subsequent success, and to sympathize with
him in his trials.

For that conspicuous public career on which he soon entered
he was phenomenally endowed. His physical organization was
attuned to every aspect and mood of nature, and was also capable

of a great amount of work and of endurance. The integrity and perfection of this organization he guarded and preserved by temperance; and, at the same time, as a lifelong advocate and example of abstinence from alcoholic and narcotic stimulants, he became a benefactor of his age and of his race.

With these physical endowments it soon became evident that there was in him a spontaneity, not only of playfulness and social entertainment, but also of whole sermons and lectures, and star-papers and occasional speeches that burst forth and rolled on to the surprise and delight of the whole country.

His pulpit began to be a point of pilgrimage for this and other lands, and to find his church the stranger only needed to follow the crowd. This continued for forty years. No such instance of prolonged steady power at one point, in connection with other labors so extended and diversified, and magnificent in their results, has ever been known.

Among these incidental labors his triumphant advocacy in England of the cause of our Union in the hour of its peril can never be forgotten. Probably the world has seen no grander instance of the ascendency of eloquence, and of the personal power of a single man, and he a foreigner, in the face of prejudiced and excited mobs. As the result of these incidental labors he became not only a social reformer, but a great factor in the freeing of the slave, in the preservation of the Union, and, ultimately, in restoring good-will between the North and the South. His name and work must, therefore, descend with benediction as an integral part of the history of the country.

In his wrestlings with those great problems of human life and destiny which have stirred thinking minds in all ages, I have wished for Mr. Beecher, as for all others, the freedom which he claimed; but have not always gone with him in his solution of the problems. On these the last word has not yet been said, and we must agree to differ. If he did not always come out right in the end, he cast light by the way, and his speculations will go in with the seething mass till the truth shall be made clear. In the mean time we look with wonder at the many-sided man and his many-sided work, and thank God for the good he has done.

MARK HOPKINS.

Williams College.

BARON BERNHARD VON TAUCHNITZ.

I FEEL indeed honored at being invited to offer a word of eulogy in memory of the illustrious American who has departed from earth, Henry Ward Beecher, whose effective work and noble services in behalf of mankind have extended even throughout the German Empire. At this time of writing, the entire press of Germany, without exception, unite in proclaiming the great loss which America has suffered in his decease, and the high merit of his work and services. Thus will the memory of this great man ever endure, not in his country alone, but also with us in the Fatherland.

TAUCHNITZ.

Leipzig, Germany.

MR. ANTHONY COMSTOCK.

WHAT pen can describe the gifts with which the Almighty endowed Henry Ward Beecher? As well attempt to count the sands of the sea or the drops in the ocean. Who can comprehend his genius? By what standard of measurement or process of description can one compass his diversity of gifts? But over and above all eloquence, genius, and powers, stands, in my mind, the grandeur of a heart so filled with love to God that he regarded all mankind as his brethren. Charity abounded to all. Malice had no place of allodgment in his heart! Misrepresentations of what he said and did were abundant. These attacks were often especially exasperating and hard to bear; and yet, over all, in his heart seemed written, " Love to God," and this seemed the key-note of peace and joy in his life.

Mr. Beecher endeared himself to the New-York Society for the Suppression of Vice and to myself by his defending and espousing our cause at various times. No amount of opposition, obloquy, or reproach which we had to encounter could daunt his courage in support of our cause. His eloquent voice more than once was heard in our behalf.

That life that went out so quietly on Brooklyn Heights disappeared as disappears the Morning Star, which sinks not down behind a darkened west. but melts away with the brighter effulgence of the rising Sun ; that life seems to whisper back the song of the angels, "Glory to God in the highest, peace on earth, good will to men !"

ANTHONY COMSTOCK.

New York City.

GENERAL JAMES LONGSTREET.

WITH sentiments of sympathy for the friends of Henry Ward Beecher. I beg to express appreciation of that genius and labor which command admiration of the people of the nineteenth century. All that can be done must fail to fill the vacuum of his leaving. even in his ripe and beautiful years, but we may hope to temper the call of Him who gives of His abundance to magnify the harvest. of measure for measure.

Peace be with Henry Ward Beecher. always ! Amen !

JAMES LONGSTREET.

Gainesville, Georgia.

LIEUTENANT A. W. GREELY. U. S. A.

THE disparity of years between Mr. Beecher and myself has given me less opportunity than many others to see and know one of America's most remarkable men. The striking point of Henry Ward Beecher's character to me was the manner in which he succeeded in making religion a matter of deep personal interest to his associates and hearers. instead of being a matter of theoretical opinion. Many of his liberal utterances of a quarter of a century seem in the light of to-day as prophetic of the changes which have been wrought in creeds and beliefs by the advance of science. Mr. Beecher's great breadth of mind and acute perspective faculties caused him frequently to avoid those seeming conflicts of science and religion which have so embarrassed other great preachers of this country.

But to me Mr. Beecher has filled a place greater for a time, if possible, than that of teacher and preacher of religious truths. I allude to his remarkable series of addresses in England, at the commencement of our great civil war. It seemed to me then that the intense fire of patriotism which burned so fiercely over the entire North had, as it were, concentrated itself in Mr. Beecher, and caused his voice to go over the entire breadth of the United Kingdom as a flame which melted or confounded all it touched.

A. W. GREELY.

Washington.

DR. BERNARD O'REILLY.

IRISHMEN at home and abroad have reason to remember Henry Ward Beecher with the most kindly feelings. He was ever ready to defend or to advocate Ireland's right to self-government, and few men denounced more eloquently the evils of British misrule in the Emerald Isle, or the chronic cruelties of landlord oppression.

BERNARD O'REILLY.

Cork, Ireland.

GENERAL OLIVER O. HOWARD.

I HAVE always entertained a special affection for Mr. Beecher. When quite a young man I once attended Plymouth Church. and the sermon he then preached affected me deeply at the time and left an indelible impression on my mind. Many times thereafter, during my life. I have had evidences of the confidence and kindness of this wonderful man of God. I have met him often in traveling, and been cheered by his apt and abundant anecdotes and by his wholesome, hearty sentiments, which, to me, were always replete with encouragement. I have sat with family friends listening to his lectures, and have prayed to God to give that manly man a long life. He has often helped me, in moments of depression and weakness, to hold up my head, lift up my heart and take courage: and this, of course, all unconsciously to himself. And so I have no doubt his strong, fearless spirit, helped by the Holy One, has thrilled and aided other men — thousands of them — who have come within the sound of his voice or the sphere of his influence. I feel his death as a great personal loss.

OLIVER O. HOWARD.

San Francisco.

REV. SAMUEL FRANCIS SMITH, D. D.

HENRY WARD BEECHER, the great preacher, whose eloquent voice has been silenced by death, is not to be estimated by any common and accepted standard of judgment. It is not right to weigh him by ordinary scales, or to define his length and breadth and height by reference to any Procrustean measure.

As a few mountain-peaks stand out against the blue firmament, in grand separation from all their fellows, so Mr. Beecher seems to have towered in lone conspicuity among his brethren. He was not greater than all, but he was distinct from all, holding a position all his own and by himself. He was intensely human, and yet he was distinguished from other men, and even from all men of his own profession. His modes of life and study and of appeal to men were peculiarly his own. He was not trained to think or speak or act in the grooves of other men, but according to his own will and following his own methods. There is a natural difference in the minds of men. They are not constructed, except in a very general way, on the same model. Some minds are iridescent, where others see only a monochrome, as the poet discovers and expresses things hidden from minds of a duller temperament. Even if it were granted that there is no such mental attribute as genius, still Henry Ward Beecher certainly exhibited mental qualities of a higher strain than one found in multitudes, even of cultivated men. With eyes ever open, with ears ever listening, he saw that which is enchanting to the eye and heard that which is attractive to the ear,— sights to which common eyes are blind, and sounds to which common ears are deaf.

Mr. Beecher's mind seemed to have inexhaustible resources, ever ready to overflow. He did not repeat himself in thought or expression. His intellect was a living stream, running with ever fresh and sparkling waters. He was like the rushing brook of spring-time, impatient of restraint, pouring wildly and luxuriantly over its banks, and flooding the furrows along its brink. His sermons were not built after the recognized rules of homiletics, but they touched the heart, and vibrated with the pulse-beat of human nature.

No truer patriot walked beneath our country's flag. He understood our government thoroughly, and loved it. In the stormy days of the war of the rebellion he visited England, and addressed many assemblies on the existing crisis. He found a dispassionate hearing, where a professed statesman or a politician would have been neglected or misunderstood. And it is safe to say that his clear statements of the nature of our government and of the crisis which prevailed had an influence to enlighten the British people, and to plead our cause before them with an efficiency and success which no words of our praise can adequately express.

The name and fame of Henry Ward Beecher have been known to every one, north and south, east and west. Perhaps no name of a citizen of this country has been held in so general regard. As a preacher and lecturer no one has been sought more eagerly or heard more enthusiastically. He has held a place in the hearts of the people rarely secured by any public man. He has spoken peace to multitudes in affliction, warning to the young, encouragement to the doubting, and hope to the despairing.

No preacher in America has had, for so long a period, so large and sympathetic an audience. And side by side with the names which shall never die,— great in speech, in action, in benevolence, in influence,— will go down to posterity the name of Henry Ward Beecher.

S. F. SMITH.

Newton Centre, Mass.

DR. EDWARD EGGLESTON.

M R. BEECHER was too large and versatile to be summed up in a few sentences. That he was, take him all in all, the very greatest of modern pulpit orators, I have always maintained, and probably there was never a pulpit orator so many-sided in his gifts. There was something colossal about him. Pettiness was utterly foreign to him; his wit, his imagination, his analysis, his vocabulary, his courage, his aims — all were grandiose. He broke with current theology, not by the critical processes of the student, but merely because it was too narrow to contain him, too restricted to give sweep to his generous impulses and large aims. He was a tree of vigorous growth, and burst the bark on all sides. For his spirit, his work, his rare genius, his unapproached greatness as an orator, his courage in great crises, I have ever had the deepest respect and reverence. He was one of those men of whom Dean Stanley speaks as belonging to the order of Samuel the prophet, — men who connect the past with the future, and make of themselves bridges for the passage of multitudes.

EDWARD EGGLESTON.

Lake George, N. Y.

MR. JOAQUIN MILLER.

S INCE the great event which shocked the world, I have listened to the public heart, and find that it beats entirely in sympathy with the illustrious dead; so that there is no need of my hand in the proposed memorial. Still, if I could lay one single granite thought toward the rearing of his tomb, such as he was wont to utter, I should do it; but I am silent before his sublime utterances. Yet, I will bluntly say this: Henry Ward Beecher was a true man, a good man, a guiltless man, if ever a guiltless man walked this earth. I lay this testimony upon his tomb proudly, fearless of contradiction. As to his goodness, his glorious courage, his divine audacity of faith in God and man, there are no two opinions now. There should not be, there shall not be, of his integrity and purity.

JOAQUIN MILLER.

San Francisco.

FOR THE LAST TIME.

(Plymouth Church, February 27, 1887.)

THE preacher's evening task was done,
   The crowd had gone away,
But something pleaded with his heart
   A little while to stay.

For him alone the organ pealed,
   For him alone the choir
Sang soft and low, in sweet accord,
   The song of his desire.

"I heard the voice of Jesus say,
   'Come, weary one, and rest'"—
What prophecy for him was there
   How little any guessed!

As lovingly he lingered there,
   Ere yet the music died.
There came two urchins from the street
   Unfearing to his side.

The old man bowed, and, lifting up
   A soiled and homeless face.
He kissed it as a mother might,
   Then turned to leave the place.

On either side the urchins trod,
   And on the left and right
A loving hand on either pressed:
   So, out into the night.

Out, little thinking as he went,
   That never any more
His willing feet should inward go
   That sacred threshold o'er.

And it was well: more fit good-bye
   No genius could devise;
No thoughtfulness of loving hearts,
   No wisdom of the wise.

5

The " little ones" had always been
  His chiefest joy and care :
With them alone let him go forth
  And God be with them there.

And down the future he shall go
  And through the enfranchised land,
A loving smile upon his lips,
  A child on either hand.

                    JOHN W. CHADWICK.

Brooklyn.

MISS LAURA D. BRIDGMAN.

I FEEL much sympathy for them that are sore afflicted with the loss of Mr. Beecher, who is in a blissful land with our blessed Saviour Jesus. He is truly happy at a holy home in heaven. I have heard much about him with pleasure and sorrow.

                    LAURA D. BRIDGMAN.

Boston.

REV. C. A. BARTOL, D. D.

MR. BEECHER was my contemporary, born less than two months later in the same year. I remember what was perhaps in Boston his earliest speech, and how ruddy, even as a red aurora, was his cheek. How full of a pleasant humor his smile! Into what a stainless air his orb seemed to ascend and shine, and wax more and more to the perfect day! If his sky was at times overcast and the morning splendor hid, it is a change which, as the world and we are made, both nature and human nature must endure. But every cloud is a fugitive, all occultation is transient, and the stars re-appear. I would fain lay the leaf my pen traces, and aught that is true in the sketch my imagination pencils, amid the blossoms on his grave, to wither in contrast with what cannot fade.

If just occasion in any matter to censure him arose, let us make the "honorable amend" of owning the plus quantity of his worth. To use a word which has been turned out of its proper scientific sense, I call him phenomenal rather than great,—a phenomenon like a meteor, a breeze of emotion, an oratorical cyclone. As statesman or theologian, he was nothing if not on the jump. Never neutral, he provoked opposite opinions at his death, yet possessed in his traits the unquestionable excellence without which no man can attach to himself such warm and so many friends, hold a million watchers in spirit with the actual crowd near his sick-bed, and draw, as sun and moon do the tides, abounding praises over his unshrouded remains.

In a common hope, we bid thee hail and farewell. Very pleasant hast thou been to me, my brother. Thy love was wonderful ; and where that is so much as was thine, the Lord in mercy still opens the door.

C. A. BARTOL.

Boston.

GENERAL NEAL DOW.

In undertaking to contribute to this memorial to Henry Ward Beecher, I am greatly embarrassed in this : that I can say nothing of him that is not already known to those who read in all languages. To say that he was one of the most conspicuous figures in America for many years; that he was one of the most influential men of his time in many ways, though never holding office; that he was one of the foremost men in the pulpit, on the platform, and in the press in influencing public opinion upon all important public and social questions, is to say only what the world already knows. All this prominence was due only to his wonderful powers of mind, which, by common consent, were regarded as equal to those of any other man of this century. Few men of our time will be remembered so long as he, and no name will go down to a more distant future than his.

NEAL DOW.

Portland, Maine.

MR. JOHN T. RAYMOND.

(WRITTEN A WEEK BEFORE HIS DECEASE.)

HENRY WARD BEECHER was a man of the people, grand, eloquent, and sublime. His fame will rest upon his being the friend of the downtrodden; the great Liberator; the one who, fearless and almost alone, began the fight, and lived to see the ranks swell into an army with victory perched upon its banners. Great patriot that he was, he proved his greatness by his readiness to soothe the vanquished by kind words and acts that endeared him to all who felt the influence of his magic power. His name and noble works will live more durable than the marble shaft that will mark his final resting-place,—a spot that will be as hallowed and loved as the tomb of Lincoln.

JOHN T. RAYMOND.

ELIZABETH BLACKWELL. M. D.

I HAVE always thought of Henry Ward Beecher as belonging to the advanced ranks of Christian warriors in the lifelong battle of right against wrong, of justice against injustice.

My first knowledge of Mr. Beecher's prowess was in the old anti-slavery struggle, when he stoutly battled for a weak and oppressed race. My later knowledge of his brave manhood is in that still more arduous struggle with the deadliest form of slavery,—the debasement of woman. I have, too, always recognized that wherever the cause of the weak, the poor, the ignorant, or the oppressed needed a strong and fearless advocate, one would always be found in Henry Ward Beecher.

The loss of such a soldier of Christ must be deeply felt in the community amongst whom he had so long dwelt, and I sincerely sympathize with their heavy loss. But we should all take courage from the joyful fact that the great moral evolution of humanity depends on no individual worker,—all the good that Mr. Beecher has done still lives, and others will bear on the standard that his hands no longer grasp.

Therefore, rejoicing in all the good work that it has been his privilege to accomplish, and believing that he still lives to carry on more, they are words of triumph rather than of mourning, words of encouragement to labor on zealously in the paths he has made plain, that I am disposed to utter. For the life and works of every good man will hasten the dawn of that brighter day whose faint, far-off gleam we already see on the distant horizon.

ELIZABETH BLACKWELL.

Hastings, England,

MR. BILL NYE.

I CAN hardly hope to add to the true and beautiful things that have been said of Mr. Beecher since his great heart was stilled. Men of all climes and all creeds have vied with each other to pay deserved tributes to his ability and his worth.

It was left for Henry Ward Beecher to demonstrate that holiness and humor might go together. He was the first preacher to discover that God made the gay as well as the grave, and to answer by his life the gloomy query, "Why should the children of a King go mourning all their days?" Mentally he fulfilled Coleridge's requirements for genius, for he carried the freshness and feeling of childhood into the powers of manhood.

Mr. Beecher not only taught the people, but he taught the pulpit that the preacher must first get near to his people and then he may mildly rebuke them. He learned the lesson of humanity by studying people more than books, and his sermons were less redolent of musty libraries than of broad fields and beautiful meadows.

While other strictly orthodox civil engineers and saintly surveyors corrected the boundaries that defined their creeds, Mr. Beecher ignored the line fences and helped himself to God's best promises whenever they unfolded themselves.

But above all else, he let the daylight into the Gospel and made it desirable. He pulled away the shutters and made the owls and vampires of superstition go elsewhere.

That is the reason he had to put folding-chairs and camp-stools in the aisles of Plymouth Church, while other houses of worship were mainly occupied by the choir. He was a human teacher talking to humanity in a language it could understand. He was among the first to discover that fun was not artificial, but made by the same hand that gave humanity the tear.

Henry Ward Beecher is dead, but his work will mark this century for ages to come. He was the apostle of peace, good-will, and good-humor, and his keen satire populated oblivion with the false and low spiritual hosts of hypocrisy. He taught this generation that sorrow will crowd itself upon us early enough and often enough without our seeking it out, but that we owe it to ourselves and to those about us to cultivate a joyous spirit.

Even in death, with the snowy-haired men and women of Brooklyn about him,—men and women who came to Plymouth first to listen to the boyish pastor of years gone by,—Mr. Beecher taught the Christian world that the gloom of the grave need not be enhanced by the somber surroundings which man's ingenuity has given to it. That is the gospel of gladness that Henry Ward Beecher came to preach, and it is the only gospel that will save those who are really worth it.

BILL NYE.

Asheville, North Carolina.

MR. EASTMAN JOHNSON.

I AM glad enough to add my name to the great and heroic things that Mr. Beecher has done and was always ready to do, and so is every citizen of this land, I am sure, who knows anything of his one single-handed enterprise in England in our time of war. For that alone any man in our northern country who has a heart will place Henry Ward Beecher's name high among our noblest heroes. I am very sensible of the sudden and immense loss to our land in the death of a great and powerful man, whose voice, truthful and strong and always for the right, whether in theology, morals, or politics, was heard in the land from end to end.

EASTMAN JOHNSON.

New York City.

HENRY WARD BEECHER.

HIS MANY-SIDED CHARACTER AND GENIUS.

EARLY DAYS AT COLLEGE.

IN college, at Amherst, Henry Ward Beecher was two years ahead of me, with twice that difference in our ages. In his senior year (1833-4), as I well remember, he roomed in the old North Dormitory, on the spot now occupied by Williston Hall. His chum was Orson S. Fowler, afterward the famous phrenologist. Spurzeheim had made a great stir in America, and had died in Boston only a little while before (November 10, 1832). Beecher and Fowler were ardent champions of the new science. Their room was set off with phrenological busts and charts. In mental and moral philosophy, Beecher then took up the phrenological terminology which he ever afterward adhered to. He localized our human faculties, emphasizing their physical basis and environment. He was also an enthusiast in Professor Edward Hitchcock's department of natural history—especially botany, mineralogy, and geology. He had a lively sense of the supernatural, but of the supernatural as revealed in natural forms and forces. He had his own way of expressing religious feeling and of doing religious work, but was always warmly on the side of whatever he considered right and manly.

It is idle to inquire what he might have accomplished in the more exact and severer studies of the college curriculum, had he been compelled, or persuaded to do his best in them. Mathematics he disliked and neglected. In the auction, then usual at the end of the college course, Beecher's copy of "Conic Sections" was put up as "a clean copy, with the leaves uncut." Of Greek and Latin, as afterward of Hebrew, he probably never tried to know much. He cared little for the niceties of linguistic scholarship. Comparative philology might have interested him had his studies led him in that direction. As it was, he cared more for comparative anatomy than for comparative philology. Political economy would no doubt have been a favorite study, had it then occupied the position it now does. Butler's " Analogy " was probably the most thoroughly mastered of all his text-books. He was far enough from being indolent, but he never worked methodically. His reading took a wide range, and he had a quick and easy way of getting what he wanted out of a book. His forte was oratory, and decidedly the oratory of improvisation. He could think, and think best perhaps, upon his feet. Storm and contradiction only made him more brilliant and forceful. He was, by all odds, the best debater of his college generation. I should be glad to know how he acquired his mastery of the English language. His style certainly suggests no one model. His genius made him an artist after a fashion of his own. He needed only a good, vigorous vocabulary. And the four books which probably helped him most in this regard were the Bible, Shakespeare, Milton's " Paradise Lost," and Bunyan's " Pilgrim's Progress."

Religiously, he had a great deal of hearty sympathy with the type of revivalism then popular. But he threw himself with special enthusiasm into the reformatory and humanitarian movements then just beginning to agitate the country. His father's " Six Sermons on Intemperance " had begun to do for one great object what his sister's " Uncle Tom's Cabin " was destined, some twenty years later, to do for another great object.

When I came to New York, as Professor of Church History, in 1855, Mr. Beecher had been eight years in Brooklyn. In the thirty or more years that followed, I could seldom hear him preach. But if the real tone and temper of a minister may be inferred from the tone and temper of his people, I have abundant reason to think well of the Plymouth preacher and pastor. It so happened that I occupied his pulpit much of the time during his absence in Europe in 1863. There must have been a good deal in my preaching to test the genuine catholicity of the congregation. But I was never more kindly treated by any people, or more generously commended by any pastor. He said he was not at all sorry the congregation had imbibed so much orthodoxy during his absence.

But his sturdy patriotism is that for which he will be longest and most admiringly remembered. Of the old Puritan stock, he was an American through and through, out and out. He had no European affectations — French, Anglican, German, or any other. He recognized in our national history a new democratic evangel. In his opinion, not Plymouth Rock only, but Liberty itself was struck by the shots that were fired at Sumter. Outside of the army, outside of the Government, no Northern man did more than he for the Northern cause. What he did for us in Great Britain, in the supreme crisis of our national struggle, can never be forgotten. Nor will it be forgotten that, when the war was over, he was one of the first, and one of the heartiest, to welcome back the returning prodigal. It was a rare, great, brave heart that ceased beating in Brooklyn on that eighth day of March in 1887.

ROSWELL D. HITCHCOCK.

New York City.

HIS INTELLECTUAL BRILLIANCY.

AMONG the general and elaborate estimates of the character and influence of Henry Ward Beecher, I should like to speak of two incidents — one of them personal — which illustrate his traits. No man in our generation was more sympathetic and helpful, more generous of time and effort. I am one of thousands who can testify to his timely aid and encouragement. At a period when he was at the height of his powers and his fame, when literally every moment of his time was engaged, when every word of commendation from him weighed (to imitate one of his own phrases) with the public a ton, he volunteered to write a preface to a little volume which never would have been published but for his suggestion. At that moment an introduction from Mr. Beecher was a prophecy, almost a guarantee, of success. I knew him then very slightly, so that his offer was an illustration of his common good-will and overflowing kindness of heart. When the book was in the press, his introduction was waited for. Mr. Fields wrote to know why it was not forthcoming, when the fact was disclosed that a long introduction had been written and sent by mail and lost in the transit. It was very annoying, and must have been specially so to Mr. Beecher, who was overwhelmed with work, had literally not a spare moment, and who felt, I have no doubt, as kindly as any author does, the disagreeableness of having to write over again a thing of that sort. But he promptly wrote and forwarded a second introduction,—a most agreeable little paper it was,— and the only satisfaction I ever knew he had in it was in saying that it was not half so good as the first.

The other incident illustrates his intellectual brilliancy. He was, I think, never dull. Even in repose, in the most unexciting intercourse, his mind played with constant lambency, glowed, one may say, with humor, and flowed along the channels of talk, a stream sparkling in the sun, without effort. But when he was aroused, his powers became of quite another kind, and there seemed to be in his arsenal every intellectual weapon ever given to man. There is no exaggeration in saying this. Mr. Beecher on the platform, and excited,—either by opposition, which roused the lion in him, or by the cause, which evoked the deepest emotions of his soul,— was a marvel. I heard him deliver once one of the foundation discourses on preaching to the theological students at Yale. It was an address of very considerable power, suggestive, reminiscent, witty, full of the wisdom of experience; but the great intellectual display came afterward, when he said that he would try to answer any questions put to him. Of all people to ask uncomfortable and insoluble questions, I suppose that young theological students, freshly familiar with all the dogmatic niceties and doubts of the books, are the most troublesome ; and Mr. Beecher, who always freely laid himself open by great breadth of statement, was a most delightful target for their ingenuity. The first question keyed him up to the keenest enjoyment of the situation. For some three-quarters of an hour he stood there, alert, excited, but never more completely master of all his powers, and replied to the questions thrust at him from every side in rapid succession,—questions of every conceivable sort, in theory, practice, and speculation. His replies were always brief, and they came as quick as a flash of lightning. I never saw before or since — for it seemed as if you could see his mind flash — such an intellectual display. He was witty, sarcastic, subtle, humorous ; his replies went to the mark like a bullet ; they were commonly the very essence of common sense. But the marvel was in the agility of his mind, turning instantly to a new question shot at him without warning, and without an instant's hesitation in his answer. The answer was not always a perfect solution; when you thought it over, it was sometimes a witty evasion which turned the laugh upon the interlocutor, but it was a flash that did the work for the moment perfectly. As he stood there all aglow, turning quickly from side to side, perfectly calm and yet nervously alive from his head to his feet, a curious smile wreathing his lips, and his eyes flaming and dancing, I thought I had never seen such a complete fusion of the physical and intellectual man. Not to debase the figure by a too suggestive simile, he was like a single man against a host, receiving and turning aside a hundred arrows on his shield, or like a juggler keeping in the air and tossing back a score of balls, with that marvelous dexterity which, even in a juggler, seems to be a half-intellectual quality. The readiness of his replies to questions so diverse, subtle, and unexpected was wonderful, but their aptness made the display altogether marvelous. So far as I know, this age could not match Mr. Beecher's intellectual brilliancy on such an occasion.

CHARLES DUDLEY WARNER.

Hartford, Conn.

HIS UNIVERSAL PHILANTHROPY.

IN attempting to write of the character and public services of the late Henry Ward Beecher, I am met by many formidable difficulties, chief among which is his almost universal recognition by the civilized world as the greatest preacher, philosopher, and humanitarian of the age. His contemporaneous fellow-citizens, young and old, are so familiar with the grandeur of his uttered thoughts — their wisdom, eloquence, and truthfulness — that to speak of them seems like anticipating the grateful tribute of another generation.

Are we, of the present day — with the memory of his transcendent affection for the entire human family, free and bondsmen, with his noble and impressive figure still standing, as it were, in our midst — fully able to speak of him with the calmness which his inspiring presence prompts? No! for it may be said that we have assisted at the making of that truly great man's history, and that it is already written on our grateful memories. If, therefore, the writer of these few lines has availed himself of the present occasion to add the testimony of his own personal admiration, it is not in the belief that he can add aught to the knowledge of the reader.

One of the most engaging beauties of Mr. Beecher's philanthropy was its universality. Unlike so many of his theological coadjutors, his humanity began far below the level of the human race, and reached the humblest animal creations. The writer enjoyed numerous opportunities of bearing witness to this beautiful characteristic. By his preaching and example, he enunciated the moral axiom that the church, through the medium of its restraining influence, cannot be better employed, in public and private life, than in denouncing cruelty, and teaching its friends and auditors to be humane.

Many there are who expatiate on the value of a human soul, and leave it to be inferred that the whole solar system, along with the lower half of animated nature, are of less importance. Years ago, a minister of the Gospel, desirous of putting a stop to an unchristian-like " sport " which flourished with peculiar persistency in his parish, requested his parishioners and their friends to attend church, on a certain day in Easter, to listen to a discourse on an interesting subject. They came, of course. He chose for his text that passage in St. Mark where Peter is spoken of as bitterly weeping when he heard the cock crow; and employed such eloquence and pathos, and made such a judicious application of the subject, that his hearers from that day abandoned the unchristian practice. Will any one say that this minister went out of his province in descanting on such a theme? Speculative points of faith are very well, but is not the best preacher he who, by his discourses, best promotes the practice of the Christian virtues? Such a man was Mr. Beecher. He held that no preacher of the Gospel should cease to denounce cruelty in every form until it was banished ; no priest should grant absolution to a cruel man until he had done penance for his merciless deeds.

Again, the patriotism of Mr. Beecher knew no bounds. It was visible in the burning imagery of his intellectual power,— in the pulpit, upon the platform, in society, even upon the very streets and highways of his country,— wherever his commanding voice could be heard. During the dark and bloody night which menaced the integrity of his nation's government, he stood like a rock upon the ocean's shore, holding aloft the glowing torch of American liberty and loyalty, making apparent to his erring fellow-countrymen the dangers which confronted them.

In assigning to Henry Ward Beecher an appropriate position among illustrious Americans, the mind is instinctively directed to that immortal group of which Washington was the towering central figure. One century of national existence now slumbers amidst the ruins of the past, without having given birth to another citizen of the colossal, intellectual, and philanthropic proportions of that great American divine whose loss the whole country realizes. Can it be safely predicted that the one upon which we are just entering will produce his counterpart? It is not permitted to us to anticipate the verdict of another century, but believing, as we do, that human genius has its finite limits, we may be pardoned our skepticism.

HENRY BERGH.

New York City.

AS A HUMORIST.

"THE gravest nations," says Landor, "have been the wittiest, and in those nations some of the gravest men. In England, Swift and Addison; in Spain, Cervantes. Rabelais and La Fontaine are recorded by their countrymen to have been *rêveurs*. Few men have been graver than Pascal; few have been wittier." So Henry Ward Beecher's humor was part and fiber of his earnestness. I think he never felt the burden of being "humorous." He was not rendered preternaturally solemn by the dreadful consciousness that something "funny" was expected of him; and so he never seemed to pump up his jokes or his light, laughter-compelling sayings. If he did,—for no man knows how much heartache a laugh may hide,—the pumping was so delicately done by hidden machinery, that the stream of his humor flowed as from a perennial fount of unfailing good-nature. He did not use his humor merely to create a laugh. It was part of his work—part of himself. It was natural as sunshine, in the social circle, on the platform, or in the pulpit; it was bright, restful, reverent, because of its very earnestness. Behind every laugh, in lecture or sermon, lay some ambushed truth that thrust itself upon you as the laughing skirmishers that lured you to its front passed away. He was a Carlyle's man, who "sang at his work, marching always to music," so that his efforts to be useful were "uniformly joyous, a spirit all sunshine, graceful from very gladness, beautiful because bright."

It was because his humor was so much an unconscious part of himself that one despairs of reproducing it. The task is difficult, and indeed is in most instances a failure ; note the many poor stories already credited to Mr. Beecher by well-meaning narrators who have attempted to translate untranslatable "Beecherisms." Take away the rest of the sermon, take away the company, the circumstances, the time, the argument or the conversation that called forth the jest or story,—take away from it all the preacher himself, and too often you have left Hamlet out of the play.

It was his gift — an uncommon one — to be humorous without being ill-natured. He preferred to laugh with a man, rather than at him. It is said of Charles Lamb, that he had suffered so much himself that he felt intolerance for nothing. Mr. Beecher had all of the gentle Elia's love for humanity that made his humor warm-hearted and tender. He could say biting things ; he could shoot hissing shafts with points as keen as the lancet's edge, that rankled where they struck like worrying thorns, when in righteous wrath he denounced a hideous wrong or assailed some great injustice ; but if ever he impaled one man for the mere purpose of making another man laugh, I never heard him, and I don't believe any one ever did. I have laughed many times at the bright, cheery humor that was always bubbling up in his conversation, but I never listened with the fearful apprehension that by and by somebody would be lanced for the amusement of the rest of us. This freedom from fear made his humor immeasurably delightful to his audiences, in the parlor or in public hall. The sensitive man, loving humor, as he dreaded ridicule, hailed Mr. Beecher's human, hearty jollity as a blessing. It is so easy to be " funny," to make people laugh, if one has a mind to be heartless. And how cordially do we all hate these keen, cynical, heartless, caustic, witty people, the free-lances who laugh and make us laugh at the agonies of the poor wretch on the wheel! But not many men can, or at least do, say good-natured things all through a lifetime of good-humor. This was the mission of Mr. Beecher's humor : to make the dark day bright ; to make the long hour short; to make the heavy burden lighter; not to make the truth more beautiful,—that cannot be,—but to catch the careless hearts of men, and their wandering thoughts, and so lead them to look at the truth and hear it. If, in righteous denunciation of national iniquity or individual wickedness, the Preacher's thrilling eloquence was a whip of scorpions, the Pastor's humor was a healing balm for every stripe when the involuntary flagellant humbled himself and cried him mercy.

ROBERT J. BURDETTE.

Bryn Mawr, Penn.

HIS BROAD HUMANITIES.

IT is the mission of death to glorify. In its presence defects, im-perfections, mistakes fall off, and what was intended comes to the light. Death wipes the dust from the surface of the mirror, enabling us to see its full brightness. So it has been in this case. Though Mr. Beecher's great services, civil and religious, have been acknowledged, yet, in many quarters, the acknowledgment has been made grudgingly, with qualification and abatement. Now it is full, cordial, unstinted. The man deserves all the praise that has been lavished upon him. He has earned his monument, whether it be a bronze statue, a library, a volume of laudation, or a devout memory in loving hearts. Even his limitations make his achievements more radiant, as showing against what restraining difficulties he struggled, and how a spiritual aim kept his current clear.

The cardinal element in Mr. Beecher's nature was feeling. He put the heart before the head. His great word was love. His crowning virtue was sympathy. Toward God and toward man this exuberant, overflowing affection went forth with a flood that was never diminished, an intensity that never cooled. God was a father, endowed with paternal attributes. Christ was a brother, to whose bosom he wished to nestle close. Man was a child, to be pitied, embraced, aided, encouraged. He disliked theology, not merely because it seemed to him barren, but because it was uncongenial to him. It could not give an account of his enthusiasm; and he disliked theories of society for the same reason. His compassion went trickling along the ground, bestowing itself on beasts, flowers, trees, herbs, with a force that swept away intellectual distinctions. This has been reckoned against him. It has been said, and with some truth, that he made little of the intellectual framework of religion; that he did not strengthen it, but rather weakened it, and broke it down. But that he forgot it, or allowed others to forget it, can hardly be said. Whenever he had occasion to express an opinion on the matter, it was essentially, though with modifications, and in popular language, the ancient opinion. He was, in belief, orthodox; but his fervid nature made it impossible for him to keep within "orthodox" lines. More a poet than a theologian, he used the speech of emotion rather than that of austere thought. He went sometimes into the cellar, but preferred to live in the upper rooms where there was light and air, literature, art, society. His service in associating religion with these things was immense. To make the great words, "God," "Christ," "the Spirit," synonymous with Love, Fellowship, Freedom, was a great achievement. To teach that Inspiration meant Truth was both noble and generous; while to bring dogma before the bar of the natural human heart more than compensated for any doctrinal laxity that he may have been answerable for.

To this strong, persuasive element of feeling may be ascribed his love of freedom of all kinds. The most prominent shape of this at the time of his coming forward was the antislavery contest. In this he was one of the earliest, as certainly he was one of the stanchest. None were braver, none so efficient as he. But his love of liberty was larger than this. It comprehended every form of emancipation—mental, moral, spiritual. This man welcomed ideas; was hospitable to new discoveries; was glad of any fresh suggestion of truth,—so glad, that he was not always careful to define its exact boundaries. He did more than enlarge the church: he brought it into sympathy with the growing thought of the age. Probably no half-dozen liberal preachers did so much as he to widen the scope of the divine activity. He had a passion for liberty. Like a great reservoir, he took in the running river, the trickling rill, the gushing fountain, the dropping rain, and gave them out in vast currents of refreshing water. Every cause that promised a larger sphere to the energies of men and women commanded his championship and secured his ungrudging advocacy. His service to the nation in its hour of darkness need not be repeated here. His service to humanity is less conspicuous, but more abiding.

To the predominance of feeling in Mr. Beecher's composition this also is due. He loved men, all men, the souls of men, especially the least fortunate, the struggling, the downtrodden. Human *nature* he could not believe depraved, whatever he might think of human *character;* and he wanted to encourage its highest aspirations, though doubtless he had a way of explaining the corruption he wished to remove, and some theory of evil not wholly inconsistent with his professed belief. Indeed, it was the soul of his endeavor to overcome the practical baseness he saw about him in the world. Evil, in his view, was an active, not a theoretical power; and it was his task not to reason about it, but to meet it. He possessed boundless resources of charity, and nothing made him so unhappy as the feeling that he was not in unison with the age he lived in. He was a true friend of the workingman, sympathizing with his hopes for a larger existence, and wishing for him a wide outlet into the intellectual world. His own intellectual gifts were enormous, and he naturally desired for all men a horizon as broad as he himself enjoyed. He had a great deal of " human nature" in him, and, of course, the possibilities of human nature seemed to him inexhaustible. A hearty, vigorous American, living in the midst of American popular life, and thoroughly convinced of the intrinsic superiority of democratic institutions, he sought to render them consistent, harmonious, and efficient. With foreign socialisms he had no sympathy; but native aspirations after a more equitable society met his cordial approval.

Mr. Beecher was emphatically a large man — in body, in mind, in heart, in soul; a forward-looking man, expectant, sanguine,

6

believing. Born and reared in orthodoxy, he kept his place, doing his best all the time to break down the limitations of the creed and the church,—accepting the broadest interpretations of doctrine, and stimulating the highest anticipations of man. His death causes a diminution of the active force that urges men onward; but, fortunately, the impulse is so steady now, so confirmed, so strong, that the departure of no one man can arrest it. Let us believe that his work was finished. The spirit of the age will miss the mighty voice that gave expression to it; but it is domesticated with us now. so that it cannot be removed. We must thank him in great measure for that.

OCTAVIUS BROOKS FROTHINGHAM.

Boston.

CERTAIN PERCEPTIONAL CHARACTERISTICS.

HENRY WARD BEECHER was one of those few great men whose minds have no element of mysteriousness about them. He could never have been a pliant courtier, perhaps not even a successful diplomatist, unless the matters to be arranged were such as could be settled to his satisfaction through open dealing and force of will. There was nothing secretive in his whole mental organization. He was free in the expression of his likes and dislikes, and his opinions were fearlessly set forth, with no thought of the possible consequences to himself. It was not, therefore, a difficult matter to acquire a knowledge of his mind and its working : his writings, his sermons, and his speeches had nothing of uncertainty or of evasion in their composition ; and though I was not often placed in close relations with him, the few opportunities I had for personal observation were sufficient, in connection with the study of his works, to give me very decided and, I hope, correct ideas of his perceptions, his emotions, his intellect, and his will in many of their most important manifestations. To discuss each of these within the restricted limits allowed would be impossible. I can only touch upon a few of his perceptional peculiarities as they were exhibited to me. His emotions, his intellect, and his will, will be understood by those who did not know him intimately, by the study of the works he has left behind him.

Mr. Beecher's *perceptions*, though perhaps not all of them developed to the fullest extent, were entirely free from the slightest degree of aberration. The organs through which these elementary faculties of the mind were brought into action were perfect in structure, and capable, therefore, of conveying to his brain correct sensorial impressions. Thus his eyes were large and his vision sound in every respect till such changes as age induces ensued; his ears were well formed, and his hearing was remarkably acute up to the last hours of his life. His other special senses appeared to be in a state of absolute integrity, and all performed their functions with that degree of physiological accuracy that can only result when not only the external organs are free from defects, but the cerebral ganglia by which their impressions are made perceptions are also normal in structure and action.

Of all his perceptions, I think his sight was the most highly cultivated and the most strongly differentiated from the ordinary type. He had particularly developed it in the direction of color. He was fond of precious stones, not because of their commercial value, but solely on account of the great pleasure he derived from their varied hues and the play of light from their facets and as it was refracted in their interior. He told me on one occasion that when a boy nothing gave him more pleasure than to take a glass prism, such as used to be hung from mantel lamps, and to decompose the sunlight into the primary colors of the spectrum on the white wall of his room. He regarded the rainbow as the most beautiful of all objects in nature, and the opal as the most magnificent and wonderful of precious stones. Red was his favorite color, and hence the ruby, the garnet, the red hyacinth were greatly admired by him. I showed him some beautiful garnets that I had dug up near Fort Defiance in New Mexico and which were as pure in color and as brilliant as rubies, and he was for a moment apparently overwhelmed with their beauty. He then told me that such objects had very much the same effect upon him as would be produced by a glass of champagne — "a big one," he added, laughing. "There is something in color," he continued, "that affects some of the lower animals and which has a corresponding influence on me, but which few people of my acquaintance seem to understand: a bull, for instance, is excited by a red flag; I have heard of a dog that was especially demonstrative toward its mistress when she wore a blue dress ; and there is an instance given by some old writer of a man who always had a fit of some kind at the sight of anything of a bright yellow color. I pity those poor people who are the subjects of that wonderful affliction, 'color-blindness'; I think I would almost as soon be totally blind as not to be able to distinguish one color from another."

Again, certain precious stones — among them the alexandrite, a magnificent specimen of which I once found him examining at Tiffany's — soothed him and disposed his mind to get rid of any little cares and annoyances that might be bearing heavily upon it. The change in hue that this remarkable stone undergoes from red to green and green to red, according as it is viewed by sunlight or gaslight, excited in him the most vivid emotions of astonishment and even of awe. He appeared to take in through his eyes some rare and mysterious emanation, which others could not perceive, but which overpowered him for the moment as the intoxicating odor of a flower will in some persons produce a kind of mental abstraction almost amounting to a state of hypnotism.

Form, whether in repose or in motion, had no such influence upon him as had color, though a horse in action or a vessel under sail impressed him strongly. I joined him one night in the box that he was occupying at the opera, where he had gone for the purpose of hearing "Faust," the music of which he greatly admired. During the performance of the incidental ballet, he turned his back to the stage. "Such things," he said, "do not interest me. I should look at those people if I cared to do so. I am not afraid, although all the house would doubtless stare their eyes out of their heads at the sight of a minister looking at a lot of ballet-girls. You tell me that there is not the slightest indecency about the exhibition, and I am bound to accept your dictum, knowing you to be an anatomist and physiologist ; but the ' poetry of motion,' as it is called, has, as such, no charm for me. I have had glimpses of ballets in my time, and I found them very tiresome. So, my dear doctor, look at those bedizened jades as much as you like, and I'll listen to the music of that waltz, while I also absorb the beauty of Mrs. ——'s jewels."

He was fond of music, and his ear, though perhaps not trained to the full appreciation of harmony, delighted in melody. "I like music with a tune in it," he said to me ; "something that I can take away with me and bring back to my memory when I am in the mood for such things." Some songs, especially when sung by women with rich, sympathetic voices and with the feeling that the subject and the music required, never failed to move him and not infrequently to bring tears. I remember how upon one occasion he told me, as the piece was being played by Thomas's orchestra, that Gounod's "Funeral March of a Marionette" caused in him such a mixture of emotions that he did not know whether to laugh or to cry.

But at the same time he was not insensible to the "harmonious crash" which is so prominent a feature in some musical composi-tions. I doubt, however, if the effect produced upon him differed materially from that caused by the fall of an immense body of water. It was grand. it was magnificent, but to his mind it was not music in its best form.

I know little or nothing of the action of Mr. Beecher's other special senses except that they were physiologically perfect. His sense of taste, though acute, was not finely developed in the direction of the appreciation of table delicacies. I sat next to him at the dinner given to Herbert Spencer, and I noticed that he ate only the most plainly cooked articles of the menu. Of wines he knew scarcely anything : sherry he could not tell from Madeira, or port from Bordeaux ; champagne he liked just to taste, but his principal drink on that occasion was Apollinaris water. His speech electrified his audience with its boldness. It was not inspired by any alcoholic beverage. It seemed to come forth almost automatically and with an impetus that originated outside of his body. I shall never forget the effect which his ringing words produced upon that audience, composed as it was mainly of hard-headed men who were not accustomed to be swayed by their emotions. They rose to their feet, waved their table-napkins, and shouted themselves hoarse, not because they all approved of the views which he then revealed to them, but because of the astounding courage. the wonderful regard for the truth as he understood it. and the almost superhuman honesty by which he must have been actuated.

WILLIAM A. HAMMOND, M. D.

New York City.

AS PREACHER AND SPEAKER.

HENRY WARD BEECHER was an American phenomenon, a genuine New Englander, a Puritan of the Puritans, an Independent of the Independents. No other country could have nurtured such a genius but the Anglo-Saxon republic ; no established church, and scarcely a dissenting chapel in Europe, would have given him a free pulpit ; while in Brooklyn he found a congregation of unparalleled liberality and unswerving devotion to the end of his life.

In his native country he occupies a place of his own without a rival. and probably without a successor, in the triple rôle of orator, patriot, and philanthropist.

There were and there are preachers more profound and more spiritual. and orators more weighty and more polished. than Mr. Beecher ; but it is doubtful whether any generation has produced a more powerful *popular* speaker in the pulpit or on the platform — a speaker who had such complete command and magnetic influence over his audience. He had an uncommon amount of common sense, wit, and humor, and a courage of conviction which defied all opposition. His imagination was as fertile as that of a poet, though he never wrote a poem or quoted poetry. His mind was a flower-garden in perpetual bloom, enlivened by running brooks and singing birds. He was always fresh and green, and rarely repeated himself. He had an inexhaustible store of apt illustrations, quick repartees, and amusing anecdotes admirably told. He was in profound sympathy with nature and with man, especially with the common people. He never lost self-control, not even under the greatest excitement and provocation, as when he faced those hostile audiences in England during our civil war. His services to his country in that momentous crisis, and to the cause of the emancipation of four millions of slaves, as well as his advocacy of temperance reform, have secured to him a permanent place of honor among the benefactors of his race and nation.

A common friend, Mr. Peter MacLeod. of Glasgow, who induced him to delay his return and to make those powerful addresses in behalf of union and freedom in 1863, told me that he prepared himself for his Glasgow speech by a sound sleep, and could not secure a hearing from the noisy assembly till he excited their curiosity by the question, "Would you like to hear what my wife told me when I left America?" Then he broke forth in an extemporary eulogy of Scotland that took the hearers captive. "'Whatever you do, Henry,' she told me on deck of the departing steamer, 'do not forget to visit Scotland.' And here I am, in the land of John Knox, of Walter Scott, and Robert Burns; the land where every valley is a battle-field, every brook a song, and every hill a poem ; the land whose memories are as bright as the stars and almost as numerous." I quote from memory and cannot vouch for accuracy.

I have myself witnessed some of his rhetorical triumphs. I sat at his side when he held a dense audience spell-bound for an hour during the General Conference of the Evangelical Alliance in 1873, in the Madison Square Presbyterian Church. glorifying the ministry of the Gospel above every other occupation. He spoke like a king from his throne. I quote the concluding sentences :

"Men say that the pulpit has run its career, and that it is but a little time before it will come to an end. Not so long as men continue to be weak and sinful and tearful and expectant, without any help near ; not so long as the world lieth in wickedness; not so long as there is an asylum over and above that one which we see with our physical senses; not until men are transformed and the earth empty ; not until then will the work of the Christian ministry cease. And there never was an epoch, from the time of the apostles to our day, when the Christian ministry had such a field, and there was such need of them and such hope and cheer in the work, and when it was so certain that a real man in the spirit of God would reap abundantly as to-day ; and if I were to choose again, having before me the possibilities of profits and emoluments of merchant life, and the honors to be gained through law, the science and love that come from the medical profession and the honored ranks of teachers, I still again would choose the Christian ministry. It is the sweetest in its substance, the most enduring in its choice, the most content in its poverty and limits if your lot is cast in places of scarcity, more full of crowned hopes, more full of whispering messages from those gone before, nearer to the threshold, nearer to the throne, nearer to the brain, to the heart that was pierced, but that lives forever and says, 'Because I live ye shall live also.'"

On the excursion of the delegates of the Conference to Washington, I happened to be in his company. We stopped at Princeton for a few hours, and as we two stepped out of the car together, we were greeted by the venerable Dr. Charles Hodge, the leading divine of the Old School Presbyterian Church, with which Beecher had little or no sympathy. As they had never met before, I introduced them to each other, and walked between them, remarking, "Saint to the right, saint to the left, the sinner in the middle." Mr. Beecher instantly replied, "Then you are the chief of sinners." Dr. Hodge smiled. We had hardly arrived in the church, when the students, who crowded the galleries, cried out, "Beecher! Beecher!" He was not in the programme which Dr. McCosh had prepared, but there was no escape; he must gratify the audience, and delighted them with a characteristic discourse. He humorously compared Princeton theology with St. John's book : " Bitter in the belly, but in the mouth sweet as honey."

Mr. Beecher was singularly free from sectarian prejudice and bigotry, and from his independent, isolated position he recognized the good in all denominations, from the Church of Rome to the Society of Friends. This catholicity was beautifully illustrated at his funeral, where in the midst of choicest flowers and evergreens an Episcopal friend read the solemn service of his church. Dr. Halliday offered a free prayer, and the quartette sang his favorite hymns of Charles Wesley the Methodist and Bonar the Presbyterian.

Theology was not the passion and not the forte of this remarkable man. Feeling this, he properly declined the honor of D. D., which his Alma Mater wished to confer on him, and preferred to be called simply Henry Ward Beecher. I heard him say once in his pulpit, " Theology is nothing but logic, stiffened and sanctified." Much of it certainly is no better, and even worse. While some divines and preachers build gold, silver, and precious stones on the one foundation of Christ, others build on the same foundation wood, hay, and stubble, which the fire of judgment will consume, but they themselves " shall be saved." Mr. Beecher described his theology in his last letter to me (1885) as " evangelical, progressive, and anti-Calvinistic." True theology should be as broad as God's love and as narrow as God's justice. Who was more meek and merciful to the sinner, even his own murderers, and yet more severe against sin than our Saviour?

The redeeming trait in Henry Ward Beecher's theology, the crowning excellency of his character, the inspiration of his best words and deeds, was his simple, child-like faith and burning love to Christ, whom he adored as the eternal Son of God, the Friend of the poor, and the Saviour of all men.

New York City.   *PHILIP SCHAFF.*

APPRECIATION OF ART.

A MONG the many tributes that have been and will be rendered to Mr. Beecher, there can be none more appropriate than that which recognizes his admiration and fondness for works of art. The versatility of his genius enriched alike his orations and sermons. Apart from their originality and grasp, they sparkle with a brilliancy not surpassed by the gems which he loved to fondle, and which answered to his mind as the thought of friend to friend ; for, to those so gifted with the power of interpretation all nature and art live as the page of an open book. This is the faculty that makes the true connoisseur. From such characters as these art looks for and receives its highest appreciation and its most generous patronage.

The common observer takes in little more than the surface of the picture. The art quality uncultivated fails to comprehend the poetic fancy or the artistic idealization. Our capabilities are not to be measured by our actual accomplishments. The hand may lack the skill to trace with pencil its images and fancies of beauty, but the poet and the artist may still be there in soul, lacking only the opportunity or the manual training. The ancient Latin proverb, that the poet and the orator are born and not made, has its verification in the pleasure and joy which their contemplation gives to those who love them.

Few men, in any age or country, have possessed so fully as Mr. Beecher that appreciative quality that tells the rapture of communion with the rare and beautiful. We recall, among his earlier popular lectures, one entitled "The Ministry of the Beautiful," the inspiration of his love for that which contributes so largely to his own fruitfulness as well as to his buoyant gladness.

Rev. Joseph Parker, of London, in a loving tribute to his friend, says: "Take him in theology, botany, agriculture, medicine, physiology, and modern philosophy, and it might be thought, from the range of his reading and the accuracy of his information, that he had made a specialty of each." The same character of testimony might be borne to his imaginative faculty and observation. He was a teacher to the multitude, and a companion to those initiated in the higher sphere of the sensibilities.

Such are the true patrons of art, who bring to the work of the artist a return more valuable than pecuniary gain or the praises of the general throng. Mr. Beecher may be regarded as having done, with pen and voice, for the culture of the beautiful, that which entitles him to be ranked high in the brotherhood of those who see things invisible to the uncultured eye. Having the ear of the common people as no other of his generation has had, he brought his love of those things as an offering to God, and Art, in his teachings, became the handmaid of Religion.

M. F. H. DE HAAS.

Brooklyn.

HIS SERVICES TO THE COUNTRY.

IF it be the duty of every one of us to disprove the saying that republics are always ungrateful, by confessing the debt that the nation owes to those citizens who have rendered it great services, then I may speak, with no fear of gainsaying, of the public life of Henry Ward Beecher — of what he has done for his country and for humanity. For he was one of those religious teachers who claim the right to apply the principles of Christian morality broadly to all the interests of society and vigorously to all its living issues.

"How hateful," he cried, "is that religion which says 'Business is business, and politics is politics, and religion is religion.' Religion is using everything for God : but many men dedicate business to the devil, and politics to the devil, and shove religion into the cracks and crevices of time, and make it the hypocritical out-crawling of their leisure and their laziness." These sentences may sound like commonplace now, but they were not so forty years ago. The kind of preaching to which they point was very uncommon when Mr. Beecher's voice first began to be heard in Brooklyn.

It was about this time that the irrepressible conflict for the extension of slavery began to wax hot ; and Mr. Beecher flung himself with all the ardor of his soul, with all the splendor of his eloquence, into the task of arousing the moral sentiment of the Christian people of the North against this national curse. Clear, positive, uncompromising were all his utterances for the equal manhood of the black man ; for all men he pleaded strenuously and convincingly, and always with magnanimous temper. The system of slavery he hated, but there was no bitterness toward the men who upheld it. He loved humanity more than he hated slavery, and the slave-owner as well as the slave was his brother. This one wise word of his illustrates his spirit, and may well be pondered by champions of other causes : "They are not reformers who simply abhor evil. Such men become in the end abhorrent themselves."

Yet he would not be recreant to the call of outraged humanity. I remember the day when from his lips flashed these words :

"I would die myself, cheerfully and easily, before a man should be taken out of my hands when I had the power to give him liberty and the hound was after him for his blood. I would stand as an altar of expiation between slavery and liberty, knowing that through my example a million men would live. A heroic deed in which one yields up his life for others is his Calvary. It was the hanging of Christ on that hill-top that made it the highest mountain on the globe. Let a man do a right thing with such earnestness that he counts his life of little value, and his example becomes omnipotent. Therefore it is said that the blood of the martyr is the seed of the church. There is no such seed planted in this world as good blood !"

Of course it is impossible for me to give any indication of the power with which these words were spoken. It seemed as if the very walls quivered with the intensity of the feeling. In the crowded church, men's eyes were blazing, and their chests were heaving, and tears were falling on the pale cheeks of women ; it was one of those exalted moments that do not often visit us on this earth. Some of the occasional sermons and addresses of Mr. Beecher, in the days just preceding the war, were eloquent beyond all words of man to which I ever listened. And the value of the service that he rendered to his country in that fierce time, and especially by his masterful speeches in England, it would not be easy to exaggerate.

This, at the least, we may say of Mr. Beecher : that with him patriotism was religion ; that he counted the service of his country as chief among the services of God ; that he filled his labor for the welfare of the State with a spirit as unselfish, as consecrated, as religious as that which inspires the martyr and the missionary.

WASHINGTON GLADDEN.

Columbus, Ohio.

HIS FAME IN FOREIGN CLIMES.

I HAVE often wished (during my peregrinations 'round and through-out the world) that the many thousands of the home admirers of Henry Ward Beecher could have some idea of his great wideness of fame, which could only be seen and known by extensive travels. Indeed his name is a household word throughout the civilized world.

While in Auckland, New Zealand, I had occasion to go into a book-store, and among the first things I saw upon the counter were the sermons of Plymouth Pulpit. I remember also on one occasion while in London, struggling to gain admission to hear the great English preacher, C. H. Spurgeon, when a man thrust me back, with the words, " I had to wait my turn when I went to hear your great Brooklyn preacher — Ward Beecher."

Near the garden of Gethsemane on Mt. Olivet there is an olive-tree ; the guide or dragoman will tell you it is known as " Beecher."

I know of scarcely a paper or book of note throughout the nations of the world in which my wanderings have led me, of high repute, in which I have not seen his sayings quoted and his sermons reported.

Whether traveling in Australia, Egypt, India, or Europe, the common questions are asked the American tourist, " Do you know Beecher? have you heard him preach? where is his power?" etc., etc. Especially was this the case while I was traveling through Great Britain immediately after he had made his great speeches concerning the situation of our country. which occurred about the close of our civil war. It is admitted by those of high rank and influence, there were never such patience, eloquence, and platform victory as were dis-played on the occasion of his speaking at Liverpool, London, and at the great Free-trade Hall at Manchester.

There is no doubt but that he turned the sentiment of England in favor of the North ; and for this great work alone the entire country should make a befitting tribute to his memory, and no doubt they will. At many of these occasions he literally compelled vast audiences (who were thoroughly opposed to his views on the subject) to listen to him until midnight ; and this, too, after having hissed him for more than an hour, before they would permit him to speak. It is commonly known and admitted that these services were of the highest importance to the country.

It seems to me that the greater part of Brooklyn has gone, since Henry Ward Beecher has left it, and in my future wanderings I shall feel lonesome — not that personally I knew him so well, but that his name was so often mentioned in my presence, reminding me of home, while yet abroad.

PHILIP PHILLIPS.

New York City

LOVE OF NATURE AND VERSATILITY.

No serious and thoughtful person could have lived in this country for the past thirty or thirty-five years without feeling in some measure the spell of the name of Henry Ward Beecher. It was a name that gradually came to stand for a great personal and intellectual force, potent not merely in theology, but in politics, in sociology, and in all national and humanitarian questions. It was a name to conjure with in war as well as in peace, in the arena of politics as well as in the precincts of the temple. Thoroughly imbued with the modern spirit, and with the American spirit, Mr. Beecher was, for nearly fifty years, one of the most considerable and active personal factors in our civilization. The influences for good, for growth, for development, for nationality, and for the formation of robust manly character that constantly went out from him in his multifarious activity, it would be hard to estimate. Not an enemy of man or of our institutions but had reason to hate and to fear him; not a good cause triumphed but had reason to thank him. His service during the war was, doubtless, greater than that of any other non-fighting man; and after the war, he was proportionately conspicuous in bringing about a real peace.

Like so many other young men, I early felt my share of attraction for this great name. The force which it represented was so broad, so human, so many-sided, that we all saw ourselves more or less fully typified in it.

I owe Mr. Beecher a debt as a student of nature. My first acquaintance with his mind was through his "Star Papers," a volume which came into my hand one summer day in 1857. This book, probably, has more literary charm and value than any other of his published works. It shows him mainly as a writer upon nature and rural themes, in which field his heartiness, his boyishness, his flowing animal spirits, his love of beauty, his lively fancy, and, above all, his solvent power of emotion and imagination which enabled him to transmute and spiritualize natural objects, had full swing. It is largely made up of short papers written during his summer vacations, from various rural towns in Connecticut and Massachusetts, and is full of the joy in rural sights and sounds which such a man has during his brief holiday in the country in midsummer. It abounds in that peculiar full-throated quality of his, that great power of articulation kept well in hand, and touched to the finest issues. What charming chapters are those upon "Flowers," "Trouting," "School Reminiscences," "A Walk Among Trees," "Building a House," "Springs and Solitude," "A Moist Letter," etc.! They are all sermons, they are all directed to the making of life better and happier; but what breezy, refreshing reading they afford! Every chapter is like an open window or an open door that lets the air and fragrance in and the eye and the mind out. Mr. Beecher's mind was not fine and compact, like those rarer products of nature, but it was large, flexible, fluent, and liberating. It was like the great, generous, juicy fruits, that bespeak the health and bounty of nature rather than her delicacy.

I first heard Mr. Beecher speak, about 1859, while living in Newark, N. J. I remember well his theme, "The Burdens of Society," and what a pouring shower of tropes and ideas the discourse was. Indeed, it seemed as easy for him to talk as for the clouds to rain, and he let himself out in the same broad, copious manner.

When a great man dies, the planet seems a good deal less inhabitable; the day seems cheaper; life seems meaner. For a long time now our politics will seem less significant that Henry Ward Beecher is no longer here to take part in them. There is no great popular question of the day but suffers in interest and importance that his voice can no longer be heard upon it. A man of action, no recluse, no saint,— a man to mold and sway the multitude and to throw out and set going all the large and generous and patriotic emotions,— he was like the earth in spring when all the streams run full. How copious, how expansive, how abounding! What a stream of sermons, lectures, talks, and writings he poured forth for half a century! He was as fluid as the sea, and could on occasion exhibit the might and the vehemence of the great elemental forces.

He was a live man, and to the last showed no tendency to become a fossil. Every progressive and liberalizing thought still found a hospitable reception in his mind, and was sent forth recruited and refreshed. A great force himself, he readily connected himself with the great currents of human affairs. Rarely did he ever mistake an eddy for the main drift. None saw more clearly which way the world was moving. He was in *rapport* with his race, his country, and his times. He was quick to see the force and the value of the theory of evolution ; he was quick to see how and when the old theology was pinching and galling the modern spirit. He drew courage and inspiration from all the renewing and expanding proc-esses of nature. He saw how the old must give place to the new, and that the young buds are formed before the old leaves fall. He was always in favor of more freedom, more air, more light. A policy of restriction, repression, and ossification he favored neither in theology nor in politics. Theories and doctrines have their day, and in all growing things there is always a demand for more room, and for fresh sources of supply. How we shall miss him in all the arenas where the triumphs of the people have been won! A great soldier in the war for the liberation of humanity has fallen. He was always a brave soldier and a conspicuous one, and always in the fore-front of the fight. Perhaps the single word that best expresses him is, multitudinous. What a multitude of ideas and impulses he pos-sessed! how wide and various his interests! and, when aroused, the momentum of his speech was like that of an armed host. And he was never more at home than when confronting a multitude of people. In these respects he was peculiarly American ; he was continental, and not insular. He was the outcome of our varied, teeming, onrushing national life. He was American in his freedom, his audacity, his breadth of view, and in his cheerful good faith. One great source of his popularity was that he represented us so well — represented our better tendencies and possibilities.

No one man is a summary of all good traits and qualities. We cannot have in so large a measure the elements of popularity which Beecher had without some drawback. The more select artistic and literary minds feel a certain want in him on the side of taste and self-denial ; and the more meek and devout religious spirits feel a want in him on the score of reverence and humility. But these defects were inseparably connected with his great merits. The work he was made to do was of a large national kind; not a service to the individual merely, but to the people ; not a service to taste, but to humanity. He was not for the edification of saints, but for the rebuking of sinners. He shed no fine poetic light, but he glowed with the warmth of all generous and patriotic impulses. He was closer akin to Luther than to Newman ; to Knox than to Emerson. His work was to secularize the pulpit, yea, to secularize religion itself, and make it as common and universal as the air we breathe. Things in closets and in corners, secluded from the light of common day, or cherished as too precious for human nature's daily food, received little sympathy from him. The saint, the scholar, the recluse, each has his place and his work ; so had Beecher his. It is very certain we shall never look upon his like again.

JOHN BURROUGHS.

West Park, New York.

AS A FRIEND OF THE JEW.

THERE have been men in history who appeared to the eyes of their contemporaries like mountains set on everlasting foundations. Henry Ward Beecher may more properly be compared to a broad river, flowing through the land, perhaps now and then overflowing, but everywhere carrying gladness and blessings on its waters. His most salient trait was his intense humanity. This trait determined his liberal attitude in religion ; this led him to espouse the cause of the slave, and made him the ready and eloquent champion of all downtrodden races.

The Jews have a special reason to pay an earnest tribute to the broad humanity of Mr. Beecher. As a result, partly of religious bigotry, partly of brute social antagonism, a feeling of indiscriminating dislike toward the Jews as a class remains among people otherwise enlightened, and from time to time finds vent in slanders on Jewish character and petty acts of social persecution. Happily the time has gone by when such persecution could take the form of wholesale massacre or pillage and torture, but the spirit of persecution still lingers on, and shows itself in a thousand vulgar ways. Mr. Beecher's large heart rebelled against persecution in any form, and toward the Jews he acted the part of a man and a brother in the truest sense.

In his sermons he did not seek to exalt the New Testament at the expense of the Old, but lovingly dwelt on the sublime teachings of Moses and the prophets, and beheld one continuous line of spiritual truth extending through both Scriptures. He spoke in glowing language of the character and services of many modern members of the Jewish people, and the utterances on this subject which are contained in his published addresses, and in his recent letter to the President, are among the most just, the most availing, and the most seasonable that have been heard for many a day. I doubt not that they will have the effect of opening the eyes of many, and that their influence will be felt for years to come.

Mr. Beecher uttered a grand thought, in his sermons on Evolution and Religion, when he said that the " moral qualities are not only divine in themselves, but are constituent letters in framing our idea of Divinity"; that we are God-builders; that if we are base and cruel, our ideas of God will be base and cruel; if we are fine and spiritual, our ideas of God will likewise be fine and spiritual. But with equal justice it may be said that the moral qualities are not only eminently human, but are constituent letters in framing our idea of humanity as expressed in others. An old proverb says, " Tell me with whom thou consortest, and I will tell thee who thou art." We may alter this proverb somewhat, and put it as follows : " Tell me what thy opinions of other men are, and I will tell thee who thou art." Our own character is the divining-rod which helps us to find the gold in the character of others.

And we may therefore regard the fact that Mr. Beecher rose so high above the social prejudices of his surroundings, and the favorable opinion which he formed of a people that is still despised by many, as an eminent testimony to the gentleness and nobility of his own nature.

FELIX ADLER.

New York City.

EARLY AND LATE IMPRESSIONS.

I FIRST saw Mr. Beecher when he came to New Haven to preach during my student days at Yale College. It seems strange to me now that this sermon made so little impression upon me. The reason was, doubtless, that I had been brought up in the Protestant Episcopal Church, and his unconventional manner in the pulpit at first repelled me; but a little later I heard him in his own pulpit several times, and became fascinated by his treatment of all subjects with which he there dealt.

What drew me most strongly to him, perhaps, was the fact that in those old days of the antislavery contest he was fearless upon the right side. Nothing had done more to undermine religious belief in me than the feeling that the Christian Church was false to its mission, in standing by slavery throughout the country. The attitude of Mr. Beecher, so fearless in the good cause, did much to counteract this feeling. Then, too, I liked him on account of the enemies he had made: certain newspapers in New-York City never wearied in pouring contempt upon him, and, very naturally, this strengthened my belief in him.

In those days, too, when the popular lecture exercised an influence, his thoughts were strongly impressed upon me and upon many of those about me in the lecture-room.

When the antislavery struggle was becoming every day deeper and stronger, Gerrit Smith once said to me, "Beecher is doing nobly: how wonderfully he takes hold of the people: I have always tried to keep one arm around the truth and then to get the other around the people, and so to bring them together; but Beecher seems to hold fast to the truth, and then get *both* arms around the people."

At a much later period, after the great struggle was ended, I saw him in a different field and from a different point of view. He came to Cornell University to preach in the course of University sermons, and I was greatly impressed by his power of stating important truths so that thinking young men could accept them, and by his readiness to throw overboard a great deal, that in these days prevents such men from giving much heed to preaching.

I have noticed in several discourses regarding him, a statement that his theology was very defective. Perhaps so, but some of his theological statements seemed to me really inspired. He seemed to have a deep insight into the great truths of religion and to be able to present these to others, opening up at times great, new vistas of truth by a single flash. There is no doubt in my mind that very many young men who had been repelled by statements of doctrine which seemed to them outworn, were brought by Mr. Beecher into a more reverent attitude of mind, and a feeling that the pulpit had a message to them after all.

His theology seemed to compare with a great deal of that which is presented in the pulpit as a bright, clear, bubbling spring compares with a stagnant pool.

The personal characteristic of Mr. Beecher which impressed me most deeply was his intense love of nature. Driving out with him on a beautiful day, over the hills looking upon Cayuga Lake, we were chatting along pleasantly, when suddenly he put his hands upon the reins and said, " Stop! don't speak a word!" and we staid there in perfect silence. I heard nothing save the whistling of a bird in the neighboring wood. We listened in silence for ten minutes, Mr. Beecher being apparently lost in admiration, when he said, " I would give a hundred dollars if that bird nested within half a mile of my house." He gave me its name and characteristics.

On another occasion he had arrived on Saturday afternoon, and at once showed much interest in the attempts to make a lawn about the University buildings. The next morning we started from my house for the University chapel, which was besieged by an immense audience. As he kept his eyes upon the ground and seemed rapt in deep thought and said nothing, I took it for granted that he was thinking over his sermon, and so I kept silence. Suddenly, as we neared the chapel steps, he came out of his reverie and said, " Yes, I was right yesterday. I have studied the grass on your grounds as we have walked along, and I am satisfied that what you need is to sow such and such kinds of grass seed in such and such proportions," naming the grasses which he thought would serve best. These words revealed the fact that on his way to meet this great audience his thoughts were not at all directed to the sermon which he was about to preach, but that he was entirely drawn away to the question of giving a beautiful herbage to the University grounds.

The last time I saw him was when he came to preach the funeral sermon of Mrs. Sage. Early in the morning before he left Ithaca, I met him driving upon the University grounds with Mrs. Beecher: he insisted upon my entering the carriage : it was a beautiful day, and his enjoyment of everything about him was that of a boy let out of school — a feeling of joy in nature such as I have never seen in any other human being.

This reminds me that General Grant once spoke to me in very hearty terms regarding Mr. Beecher, and said, " Beecher is a great, noble-hearted boy."

To me Mr. Beecher seemed always a born poet. In another country, and in other times, he would probably have influenced men as a poet rather than as a preacher.

ANDREW D. WHITE.

Cornell University.

SYMPATHY WITH THE SHAKERS.

To UNDERSTAND the light in which the Shakers viewed Henry Ward Beecher, it is necessary to know somewhat of their very peculiar theological beliefs. Therein it will be seen that whereas Mr. Beecher was heretical to Church and State orthodoxy, he was orthodox to Shakerism.

The writer, in company with Elder R. Bushnell, visited Mr. Beecher in Lenox, Massachusetts, some fifty years ago ; and Mr. Beecher several times visited Mount Lebanon ; views were on these occasions freely interchanged, and theological points discussed. Whilst Mr. Beecher was a believer in Christ's first appearing, the Shakers believe in the first and *second* appearing of Christ. The Shakers claim that the Bible is not the word of God, but an imperfect record thereof ; that the God of the Jews was not the very Deity : that Jesus was not the very Christ : that Christ is a spirit from the seventh or Christ heaven — the heaven of heavens. From that spirit sphere go inspiring angels to prophets and prophetesses, in all nations and races, on all the earths in God's unlimited universe of inhabited globes.

That man's probation extends into eternity; that the physical body knows no resurrection — dust to dust; that God is a dual Being — a heavenly Father and heavenly Mother; that celibacy, community of goods, and non-resistance or peace are elements of pure, unadulterated Christianity. There are many phases of Christianity, from rebel Chinese Christianity up to Shakerism; in all of them there are some truth, some good, and some salvation. These are some of the elements of the Shaker theological beliefs which Mr. Beecher "looked into."

How many of these doctrines Mr. Beecher incorporated in his sermons is an interesting inquiry; but we know that, under the inspiration of the "Christ angels," he preached many a good orthodox Shaker sermon. He preached salvation of body as being included in the salvation of the soul; and he recognized Jesus — a perfect Jew — as the highest type of physical beauty that our race ever produced. As did his father before him, he preached and practiced health as a Gospel virtue; believing that, in obedience to physical law, the Lord our God will yet take away all sickness from the midst of his people. Mr. Beecher was a John the Baptist to Christ's Second Appearing — Shakerism.

Like Theodore Parker, Mr. Beecher assimilated more with the Shakers than with any other religious body of people. He taught abstract truth as the people were prepared, saying that " a preacher who should preach all the truth would be like a bull in a china shop." Shakers attended his church, and read his sermons in their assemblies perhaps more than those of any other preacher. None but a cordial, friendly, personal relation existed between Henry Ward Beecher and the Shakers, who regarded him as a large-hearted humanitarian; a generous, liberal-minded theologian; a prophet of good things to come to the whole human race — a John the Baptist, not to some individuals, but to a dispensation.

In the following particulars I understood Mr. Beecher to more or less perfectly agree with the Shaker theology:

In the Motherhood as well as the Fatherhood of the Godhead.

That the saints will inherit the earth as an inalienable right.

That land-monopoly is the basis of chattel and wages-slavery.

That salvation of body is included in salvation of soul.

That the physical resurrection is a physical impossibility.

That man's probation is eternal, and that he creates his own heavens and hells.

That other Avatars, or Messiahs, than Jesus have been inspired by Christ angels.

That the Bible is an imperfect record of the word of God.

Upon these points of Shaker theology, I believe, Mr. Beecher and the Shakers were at agreement.

Mr. Beecher inaugurated a theological war that has spread throughout all church organizations in America and England. Himself he "ordered the battle," but he summoned "the young men of the princes of the provinces" to do the fighting. The battle having been fought and the victory won, Mr. Beecher was no longer needed. But he has left a whole army of Beecher veterans who are far more to be dreaded by orthodox Church and State Christendom than its leader was ever to be dreaded.

The new generation of Beechers will greatly enlarge the boundaries of rational Revelational Theology : and, Sabbath by Sabbath, the people will go to hear new truths from the young Beechers that will end in abolishing wages-slavery. As Mr. Beecher loved congregational singing, so will his spirit rejoice in the congregational preaching yet to be established in the Brooklyn Beecher Church.

To me, Mr. Beecher was like the saints and prophets of previous dispensations, of whom an apostle said, "These all died in faith, not having received the promises — the fruition of their own hopes and predictions ; God having provided some better thing for us, that they without us should not be made perfect."

Henry Ward Beecher is not yet ascended into the seventh heaven ; he is not yet glorified. His work is not finished ; "being dead, he yet speaketh" and worketh. But he will stand in his lot, with Moses and Elias, and with David, who "hath not ascended into the heavens" ; and with the "souls under the altar," who are waiting for Christ to make his Second Appearing to those who are, and shall be looking for him, without sin, unto salvation.

F. W. EVANS.

Mount Lebanon, N. Y.

REMINISCENCES AND INCIDENTS.

MR. E. P. ROE.

IT was not my privilege to enjoy an intimate acquaintance with Mr. Beecher, yet I can recall some scenes in which he was a central figure. On one occasion he and a large party of friends made an excursion in the Catskills and returned in the evening to the Tremper House. As one of this party, I had opportunities of conversing with him and of listening to his felicitous speech at supper. Dr. Bevan, formerly pastor of the Brick Church in New York City, was also present. With a number of clergymen he had dined with me a few days before and had told a capital story most admirably. I knew that if he and Mr. Beecher could be brought together on the hotel piazza, they would, metaphorically, " make sport which would bring down the house." (I hope the illustration will be pressed no further.) By a little management, this conjunction was arranged. Mr. Beecher enjoyed Dr. Bevan's story in his hearty way, meanwhile being fired up himself, and a corruscation of wit and fun resulted not easily forgotten. He was surrounded by a large group of clergymen and their wives who were in sympathy with him as he with them, and so he was beguiled into one of his best and most brilliant moods. Shouts of laughter rang out on the still June evening, and the hilarity of that hour was as good as a week's vacation to the hard brain-workers present. In his genial, overflowing humor, this many-sided man was a beneficent power.

Again when on a brief journey with Mr. W. Hamilton Gibson, the artist, I met him in the cars, and was interested in noting how perfectly at home he was on artistic subjects and works.

My most memorable interview occurred one June day when Mr. Beecher, with a number of Congregational clergymen, visited the Rev. Dr. Abbott at Cornwall-on-the-Hudson. The party landed at West Point, and Mr. Beecher was put in my carriage and sat on the same seat with me in the drive over the mountains. At times he was like a boy just loose from school in his frolicsomeness; again he would show his deep sympathy for nature. He fairly reveled in the scenery, and knew the names of the trees and plants on which his eyes dwelt in fond appreciation. He was as much at home in the Highland solitudes as when electrifying thousands by his eloquence. In brief, he was one of the few to whom genius gives the power of almost unlimited insight and adaptation.

E. P. ROE.

Santa Barbara, Cal.

DR. GEORGE H. HEPWORTH.

WHEN I was pastor of the Church of the Messiah in New York City, the conservative current in my character carried me out of the ranks of Unitarianism and landed me — nowhere. I simply knew for a time that I had left my old religious home and was out on the broad prairie without shelter. It was a terrible experience, the nervous shock of which I cannot even yet, after fifteen years, contemplate without an involuntary shudder. One morning my door-bell rang, and three cards were handed to me by the servant. My visitors were Dr. William Ives Budington, Dr. Henry M. Storrs, and Mr. Beecher. I was so blue about myself, and so dazed by the fact that I was all afloat, adrift from my moorings, that my first impulse was to excuse myself, and remain hidden in my den. I shrank from all human companionship.

Still, I entered the room where these three gentlemen were seated, and was surprised at the greeting I received. Mr. Beecher saw my condition of mind at a glance. His intuitions were something marvelous. How he did talk to me! with what tenderness and brotherliness and gentleness! And withal, how full of keen wit and quaint and odd remarks his conversation was! I just sat there and listened, hardly replying by a word. I felt like " a sensitive " when the mesmerist makes the mystic passes. He promised for himself and for the other two brethren, and for the religious body which he represented, to stand by me as something more than a friend, as a brother, until I could see my way and my duty more clearly. And he kept his word. He was my good cheer at a time when old friendships had suddenly given away, and no new relationships had yet been formed. "I will be your bishop," he said.

The old days come back as I write, and with painful vividness. I had a great burden to bear, but Mr. Beecher put his shoulder close to mine and helped me more than I can tell. I can never forget those weeks and months. But they were cheered, inexpressibly cheered, by the man who did a thousand acts of kindness like this one, but will never be known until we all shall reach another land.

GEORGE H. HEPWORTH.

New York City.

MR. MELVILLE D. LANDON ("Eli Perkins").

MR. BEECHER will never be called a humorist, but his wit and humor was as keen as his logic. He never strayed away from his train of thought to gather in a witty idea to illustrate his sermons. Neither did he avoid wit. When a witty idea stood before him, he grasped it, and bent it to illustrate his thought. His conception of wit was as quick as lightning. It came like a flash (often in a parenthesis), and it often instantly changed his hearers from tears to laughter.

When some one asked the great preacher why the newspapers were always referring to the Plymouth brethren, but never spoke of the Plymouth sisters, he could not help saying:

"Why, of course, the brethren embrace the sisters!"

Mr. William M. Evarts was once talking with General Grant about the great Brooklyn divine, when suddenly the distinguished lawyer musingly asked:

"Why is it, General, that a little fault in a clergyman attracts more notice than a great fault in an ordinary man?"

"Perhaps," said the General thoughtfully, "it is for the same reason that a slight shadow passing over the pure snow is more readily seen than a river of dirt on the black earth."

In all of his humor. Mr. Beecher never harmed a human soul. His mirth was innocent, and his wit was for a grand purpose.

The kind heart of Mr. Beecher, and the effect of his sweet life upon humanity, can be no better illustrated than by a little incident which happened one cold, wintry morning, as the kind-hearted preacher was buying a newspaper of a ragged, shivering Irish newsboy.

"Poor little fellow!" sighed the sympathizing clergyman, while his eyes moistened, "ain't you very cold?"

"I was, sir, before you passed," replied the boy.

MELVILLE D. LANDON
("Eli Perkins").

New York City.

DR. EDWARD EGGLESTON.

NONE who ever knew Mr. Beecher will ever forget his exuberant playfulness or his flashing wit. In playfulness he sometimes disregarded conventional restrictions ; but if you will have a great man, you must expect the slender fences of bourgeois properness to be now and then overturned. He often twitted me in many ways on my excessive head of hair. " You shaggy man, come up here," he called to me one Friday evening as his prayer-meeting was breaking up. In the severe ordeal of his trial, he one day sent two notes to Pastor Halliday, who sat next to me. One of the notes warned him that he was sitting alongside " a dangerous man. He is an American! Witness the growth of his hair ; a soil that produces such a crop is over-rich — malarial indeed!" The other note warned Mr. Halliday : " The fires of Calvinism have burned all the hair off of your head. Look at your neighbor, and learn a more liberal faith." And this in the very midst of one of the most exciting periods of the trial.

EDWARD EGGLESTON.

Lake George, N. Y.

MR. ANDREW CARNEGIE.

THE desire of every visitor to our shores, whether philosopher, poet, historian, physician, or statesman, to hear Mr. Beecher often led me to Plymouth Church. Matthew Arnold was no exception to the rule. After service, Mr. Beecher came direct to us, and as I introduced him, he extended both arms, grasped the apostle of sweetness and light, and said, " I am very glad to see you, Mr. Arnold. I have read, I think, every word you have ever written, and much of it more than once, and always with profit." Mr. Arnold returned Mr. Beecher's warmth — as who could ever fail to respond to it?— and said, " I fear, then, you found some words about yourself which should not have been written!" " Not at all, not at all!" was the prompt response, and another hearty shake of both hands, for he still grasped those of his critic. " Those were the most profitable of all."

Upon another occasion I had gone with a well-known English divine to Plymouth Church, and in the party was Miss Ingersoll, whom I introduced to Mr. Beecher, saying, " This is the daughter of Colonel Ingersoll; she has just heard her first sermon, and been in a church for the first time." As with Mr. Arnold, the arms were outstretched at once ; and grasping hers, he said, as he peered into her fair face, " Well, you are the most beautiful heathen I ever saw. How is your father? He and I have spoken from the same platform for a good cause, and wasn't it lucky for me I was on the same side with him ! Remember me to him."

ANDREW CARNEGIE.

Pittsburgh.

MRS. JESSIE BENTON FRÉMONT.

OF Mr. Beecher in his more public life many are writing from larger knowledge, and those who knew him closest tell what can be known only to unreserved friendship; but I have one quiet recollection of him, so characteristic, so fine, that if I had but that one it would be enough to explain the devotion of those who realized constantly his quick sympathy and his generous consideration for the feelings of others. We are on guard against great tests, but the surprise of a sudden small stab finds out the vulnerable point, and reveals us as we are : our nature and that habit of mind which has become second nature is suddenly uncovered, sometimes to our own dismay, sometimes to our own approval. It was in such a way that I saw Mr. Beecher tested by a Southern lady, who intended giving public recitations, and had asked me to have him hear her recite, and give his opinion as to her voice. Had it been a case of merit and necessity I should have felt less unwillingness to tax his time, but there was little merit, and absolutely no necessity. She was a widow with two little children, but for herself and her children both their future and present were made luxurious and secure. Her husband's income died with him, but her family had large wealth and generous affection, and every detail for her comfortable independence, even to a good income, was securely provided. They were not only people of large estates, but proud of their historic, honored name : and Mrs. B. was not let to feel any loss they could remove. She was unusually lovely, with a gentle, appealing, helpless manner which enlisted protecting feelings. "She is so sweet, so gentle!" was a chorus that always followed her.

But this sheltered life of obligatory retirement from society developed the vanity, the need for excitement which underlay this sweet delicacy, and her family were justly indignant when, with the invincible obstinacy of an unreasoning mind, she decided to give public recitations. "I must have bread for my children," was her phrase — as senseless as that of a parrot. She had no conception of the anguish of those words — the crowning agony of the widowed mother.

Nor had she the remotest doubt of success, or any idea of what lay in her way to public fame. A vision of a lovely, tall, fair woman, in long mourning robes, reciting melodious verse to an audience who pitied and admired her — that, and only that, she saw.

In short, her people having ineffectually pleaded and argued, she had escaped from them all, and had now come to New York to arrange for her début. There was old friendship between our families, and my feeling was to protect hers from reproach.

I brought her to my own house, where I invited critics and managers to hear her read, and they kindly humored her with praises, aiding me to gain time until her sister should arrive, who had answered me, begging I would keep Mrs. B. amused until she could be ready to take her to Europe. But restlessness made the elocution lessons a bore. "Professional" opinion, she said, was commonplace and hackneyed ; she wanted some great orator, some speaker of distinguished success to hear her—that would be a true opinion. And she had fixed upon Mr. Beecher. Hence came my unwilling request for a brief visit to him that a Southern friend of mine might have his opinion of her voice — that she intended giving public recitations — and I gave her honored father's name.

Of course this brought the kindest answer, and next morning we were punctually at his house—the Columbia Heights house with the grand view. Coming quickly into the drawing-room to meet us, his step and smile seemed arrested by astonishment, rising to dismay, as his instant perception took in the true Mrs. B. She, sweetly, and without emotion, calmly explained her object in claiming his attention, and made her routine little speech about getting bread for her children.

It is hard on any man of feeling who tries to lift the real distress around him to meet real need. To Mr. Beecher, whose keen sympathies vibrated with the pain of others, whose daily duties were to minister to care and suffering, it brought a shock to see this lovely woman, in perfect health, and calm even tone of mind, her costly artistic mourning and unfailing bunch of white roses in her belt, conveying no thought of want or loss, no comprehension of the heart-breaking words she used so smoothly and gently of "getting bread for my children."

I think I know what he *felt ;* he *said* nothing, but, taking refuge in movement, led us to the upper library where we would be uninterrupted ; that sunny room where, opposite, was the great city, and close below the harbor with its crowded life of shipping, its ceaseless grand effort from land and sea.

On this rose the small voice of self-importance as Mrs. B. chose out from the volume handed her by Mr. Beecher, " my favorite verses," she said; and of all written words proceeded to give, in her soft, flattened tones, Shelley's "Skylark."

Mr. Beecher had mastered the first shock : this second one made him half-rise from his chair, but with his flashing-quick perceptions the wound to his ear was lost in the waves of astonishment and pure fun that overran his mobile countenance. By the time the gentle execution was ended he had, however, controlled himself. He assured the lady that " her voice was remarkably sweet, soft, and fitted to express tender feeling, but that practice under a good trainer of the voice *was* essential."

" But I would rather read with some one who was not a hackneyed trainer," interrupted Mrs. B. " I would like to hear how *you* read the Skylark."

For a brief pause Mr. Beecher was quite still. He evidently passed into another atmosphere. Taking the little book, but with his eyes dreamily looking out of the sunlit window to the blue Mayday sky, he followed in feeling as in words the song of the lark — not reciting, not reading — but giving fit utterance to its spiritual questionings and longings.

It broke upon the charmèd air to hear Mrs. B.'s conventional mild thanks for his " patience and kindness." " Not at all," was the hearty answer : " I am glad to do it for you. You have my permission to refer to me, and to use my name, publicly, for all I said of your voice."

" Oh, no, I never could do that ! " she answered, more emphatically than she was used to speak. " You see I am Southern : all my family would be shocked to find I had been to see you. It would injure my prospects in the South to use your name. I only wanted your opinion for myself."

Mr. Beecher bowed silently,—it was that battle-year which made us comrades with him, 1856.—but gave a kind smile and nod of the head to me as he saw me blushing to tears and dumbfounded by such unconscious, tremendous rudeness and selfishness.

He offered us some flowers, which she accepted with graciousness, while I brought away this lasting memory of a look deep into the springs of a large, sweet nature : his generous sympathy, his quick mastering of surprise and disapproval, his tolerance and pity for so much weakness, his escape from belittling ideas into the upper air of noble thought, his inborn goodness of heart, which made him unwilling to wound even in just retaliation.

JESSIE BENTON FRÉMONT.

Washington.